1

Rider: The Imminence

ISBN-13: 978-1480270381

ISBN-10: 1480270385

For my father, Larry Smith.
Thanks for your encouragement on this tale.

Thanks also to Larry Ivey for his time in proofreading.

Joe Palotas is a highly talented local artist. To learn more about his works, please visit ArtsInWonderland.Com.

By the same author:

"A Geeks Life"

"Meg Hunter"

"Pilgrimage of the Phoenix, Trilogy Edition"

Contact The Author At:

MegToothMan@Yahoo.Com

On Facebook At:

Michael Smith - Author

"Not all who wander are lost."

– J.R.R. Tolkien

Forward

One year later.
Jacksonville, Florida.
10:52 pm.

Twenty two year old Prett Hastings parked his car two blocks away and walked back towards the convenience store. After the robbery he figured he could cover the distance in roughly two minutes, or less if the adrenaline was pumping full bore.

And he kind of felt like it already was.

He absently wiped a sheen of sweat from his brow, despite the cool evening, then reached into his jacket pocket and grabbed the butt of the gun. It wasn't a real gun, but it looked real enough, especially after he'd pried the little red piece of plastic from the end of the barrel.

In the eyes of the law though, it didn't matter if the gun was real or not, armed robbery was armed robbery. That the gun was made in China at a toy factory called Trico Toys and came in a colorful package with smiling kids on it would not sway a judge

7

to leniency.

Prett arrived at the little strip mall and, after crossing a patch of scrub, arrived in the alleyway behind the building. The convenience store, called Skyway Market, was at the opposite end of the long, low building and Prett read the names on the back doors of the other businesses. John Franks, D.D.S., Howard Thull, P.A., Penny's Caribbean Cruises, and Pak and Sak, "For All Your Shipping Needs!" And then he arrived at the last door, the one for Skyway Market. He looked back the way he'd come, but saw nothing but blue Dumpsters and oversized plastic bins for recycling. There were also a few plastic bags laying about, but there was no wind to move them around. The damp night was quiet and still.

He stood in the darkened alleyway for a moment, wiping more sweat from his brow. There were several lights in the alley, not overly bright, but bright enough to make him feel like a helicopter search light was on him. He then proceeded to the end of the building, slipped around the corner, then leaned against the wall.

There were no lights on the side of the building, and several palm trees blocked light from humming sodium-arc street lamps, so Prett felt a sense of security in the darkness. Beyond the the front of the building and the gas pumps was Bay Road, but it was quiet at this time of night.

The town of Skyway, on the outskirts of Jacksonville, was an affluent, wealthy town of mostly retired seniors. At this time of night most of them had retired for the evening, hence the roads being quiet and Skyway Market closing at eleven instead of midnight or later.

This is one of the reasons Prett had chosen this particular store to rob, that and he knew affluent seniors tended to carry a lot of cash. The register drawer was likely to be a hundred dollar bill smorgasboard.

He took several deep breathes, then, with his right hand still on the butt of the gun in his pocket, he used his left hand to rake through his short, fair hair. His heart, while not exactly racing, was pumping blood faster than its normal rate, which wasn't helping calm the adrenaline and the slight shake in his hands.

Prett looked at his watch and the little glowing green numbers said 10:58. Two minutes till closing. Two minutes till Skyway Market locked their doors for the night. Two minutes to make a final decision that, if he were caught, would probably mark him for life.

He took two more deep breathes, squeezed the gun butt tight, steeled his jaw, pushed off the wall and headed towards the front of the building.

But he never made it. Didn't even make it two steps.

What happened exactly was unclear to Prett. One moment he was walking, then he wasn't. One moment he was heading towards the front of the mall, now he was lying face down on the road behind it, the one he'd parked his car on just two blocks away. His only intervening memory was a loud bang, as if someone had clapped their hands behind his head, and then a blinding light that seemed to come from everywhere at once.

Now he was lying on the road, his right cheek digging into the still-warm asphalt and road grit in his mouth. The smell of tar permeated his nose.

But his contemplation of what had happened was quickly supplanted by the realization that he could not breathe. The reason for this, he discovered after opening his eyes and peering over his shoulder, was because a man was sitting on his back.

The light was dim out on the street, but despite this, Prett could make out a hat atop a head full of hair and a face hidden behind a beard, the length of which he couldn't determine from his current position. He also could see two massive arms laying across knees.

Prett struggled a bit, not to try to get away from the huge man, which he thought would pretty much be impossible, but just to try and satisfy the demand of his lungs.

The man looked down at Prett, long hair rustling against his leather jacket, and seemed to notice his breathing conundrum.

He resolved the issue by leaning forward slightly, allowing Prett to take a deep breath.

"Prett, Prett, Prett," the man said in a deep, rumbling voice as he shook his head. "Twenty two years old and about to risk years' worth of incarceration. And for what?"

Prett didn't respond. While breathing was now going well, he didn't think talking would go very smoothly, especially with his face and jaw pressed against the pavement.

The man looked back down at Prett and said, "I'm going to get off you now and stand up, try and run and I'll knock you back down again. And I won't be so gentle the second time. Got it?"

Prett couldn't nod, but he issued a grunt that he hoped passed for a yes. Leaning forward, the man put his hands on his knees and pushed himself erect, then turned around. "There's a curb behind you, get up and go sit on it."

Prett did in fact debate running, but then complied, pushing himself off the ground and quickly moving to the side of the road and sitting on the yellow-painted concrete. He didn't look up at the man, instead, while panting, he rubbed sand and grit off his face and asked, "How did I get here, on the road?"

"Neat trick huh?" was the man's only response.

Prett then looked up at his captor and the first thing he noticed were his eyes. Even in the weak light they shone a blue like he'd never seen before, and he found it difficult to look away from them.

"Name's Rider, by the way," the man said and hooked his thumbs through belt loops.

Prett nodded, but said nothing. Momentarily taken aback by the color of his eyes, Prett also had trouble grasping the size of him as well. He stood well over six feet and surely weighed far north of two hundred pounds. Prett had met football players that were bigger, but somehow this man seemed to take up more space than just his physical presence.

The man who called himself Rider, besides wearing a rather beat up Fedora hat, also wore an equally well-worn brown leather jacket over a Led Zeppelin t-shirt. Only the trademark font of 'Le' and 'lin' were visible though, due to an unkempt but impressive beard that hung almost to his belt buckle.

The belt and buckle supported faded jeans that covered the tops of what looked like newer, and expensive, black boots.

"You gonna just stare at me all night, or answer my question?" Rider asked.

Prett, having now caught his breath, looked up at the man's eyes again. "What?"

"I asked you why you were willing to risk incarceration."

"Oh, I –," Prett started, then hesitated. He looked away from Rider and down at the street.

After a moment, Rider asked, "Do you want me to sit on you again?"

"I – I needed the money," the young man said, almost at a whisper.

"You don't have a job?"

Prett nodded. "It's only part time, not enough pay," he replied, then asked, "how'd you know my name?"

Rider ignored his question. "What do you need the money for?"

Prett looked up at Rider for a moment, then back down at his shoes. He absently fiddled with the laces. What was at first confusion and fear was quickly fading to embarrassment and he could feel warmth growing in his cheeks. "I – like to draw. Wanted to submit some pictures to an art show."

"What kind of show?"

Now his forehead was getting hot. "It's by – um – the Comic Book Artist's Guild."

"And how much is the entry fee?"

Prett took a deep breath and exhaled slowly, then absently rubbed his cheek again, dislodging a piece of grit he'd missed earlier. "Twelve hundred dollars, for up to ten submissions," he explained, shaking his head. He started to say something else, but his eyes froze on a sight coming down the road.

It was a motorcycle, though it looked more like a freight

train on two fat tires. Shining red paint and bright chrome winked and twinkled in what little light there was and the name Triumph was emblazoned on the fuel tank.

But this isn't what stunned Prett. The fact that the motorcycle was moving down the road of its own accord, very slowly, is what made his eyes wide. The engine was not running and the only sound it made came from the tires rolling over bits gravel and a few leaves.

Rider followed Prett's gaze and after a moment, turned back. "Don't mind the Lady, she's just showing off."

"But – it's – how –," he stammered, looking back and forth between Rider and the driverless bike.

But Rider ignored the young man's bantering. Instead he reached into his coat pocket and pulled out an envelope, then tossed it to Prett, who caught it with two hands.

"I've seen your drawings, Prett. The work you called 'Belatara' is pretty amazing, no way I could draw something like that. Then again, I'm just a motorcycle man, not an artist. But who knows, Prett, you could be the next Stan Lee or something," Rider said encouragingly, then unhooked a thumb and pointed to the envelope clasped in Prett's hands. "That's your entry fee, twelve hundred dollars. Consider it a gift, just pay it forward some day."

Prett, momentarily forgetting the motorcycle, looked at

the crisp, white envelope, then back up at Rider. *"If you already knew about the show, then why'd you ask me?"*

Rider took a long step backward to make room for the motorcycle at it slowly rolled between them. *"To see if you'd be honest with me."*

"Hold on, my work isn't even available to the public yet, it's not even published," Prett said and stood up. *"How have you seen my work?"*

Rider smiled, or so Prett thought, it was hard to tell with all the beard and mustache hair. *"Not important, Prett. What is important is that you don't make a career out of robbing convenience stores."*

As the motorcycle came to within reaching distance of Rider, he reached and plucked a helmet from the rear view mirror. *"Time for me to go,"* he said, and removed his hat, which was unceremoniously rolled up and stuffed into a saddlebag, then he started to put the helmet on.

"Wait," Prett said, raising the envelope in his hand. Rider paused and looked at the young man. *"Why are you doing this?"* Prett asked.

Rider seemed to think on this for a moment, then answered, *"A year ago a group of people gave me a second chance. I pay it forward whenever I can."*

Prett lowered his hand. *"Why? What did you do?"*

Rider lowered his helmet while maintaining eye contact, then he placed one hand on the motorcycle's seat and said, "Stop."

To Prett's amazement, the bike froze in place. He thought surely it would just fall over, but it didn't.

"I did something I was not supposed to do," the big man explained, "even though it was done for the greater good."

"What did you do?" Prett repeated.

Rider paused before answering. "I killed myself," the motorcycle man said, and with that, he pulled his helmet on and buckled the chinstrap, taking care not to entangle his beard hair.

Then he mounted the now motionless bike and placed his hands on rubber grips, then placed his boots on footpegs. Prett noticed there were no keys in the ignition, but the bike started anyway when the rider pulled the clutch handle in.

Rider tapped the transmission into first, gave the engine some gas, let out the clutch and forward momentum was taken over by a few of the over one hundred forty horses. Rider gave Prett a two-finger wave as he drove away and eventually disappeared down the darkened road.

Prett watched the darkness for a long time as he thought over the last five minutes of his life. Then he opened the envelope in his hands.

Twelve one hundred dollar bills.

Prett looked at them for a moment, then shoved the envelope into his pocket as he looked again into the darkness where the rider had disappeared.

*"Bet he's got heckuva story to tell," he said quietly, then pulled his keys out and walked back to his car. As he walked, he thought deeply about creating a new drawing for the show, a drawing called "*Rider.*"*

1

June 8th, 2014

Tampa, Florida

1:30 am

I did not choose this path in life, rather, it seems to have gleefully chosen me. I do not know if the *Imminence* is a gift, or if I am its puppet, but I don't think on it overly anymore, it serves no purpose. I know that it is not my enemy, that much I can attest, but the things it requires me to do have impacted my life in ways I cannot understand, much less express.

Like shooting a six year old girl in the face with an M249 machine gun. At cyclic rate of fire, that's thirteen rounds per second, and I pulled a two second burst. That's something you just can't pick out of your mind and dispose of, never to think about again.

It's like stepping in a pile of dog crap with brand new shoes right in your own front yard, and you don't even know of a dog anywhere in the neighborhood. So you sit down with a stick, or a toothpick, and you try to pick it all out, but some is always going to remain, no matter what you do. No matter how hard you try.

In my late teens I looked to the future and saw gold. I dreamed of getting from cradle to grave without screwing up my life too badly along the way. I had dreams. I had courage. I had the will to tackle anything life threw in my path.

And yet, now, fifteen years later, I'm just a motorcycle man. I should be dead many times over for my actions, but yet still I ride; I still roll down the endless asphalt highway. Perhaps it is the *Imminence* that keeps me alive, perhaps it is luck; it's certainly not because of my looks, which some describe as scruffy with a side of slovenly, but that's not important here.

I'm just a man who's decided to call the highway his home with a growling 1975 Triumph Trident between his legs. The road rolls beneath my wheels as they pull blackish-gray asphalt from the future, into the present, and out to the past. And sometimes the present isn't a pretty thing. But the present always fades into a sepia-colored past and, while nobody likes to see the Clearing that marks the end of our time in this world, sometimes time passing us by is a welcome thing.

Especially for me.

I do not seek out the troubles that seem to find me. Sometimes we find trouble, and sometimes trouble finds us, but suddenly it's there and you've got to find a way out. I have tried to stick to my mantra of getting from cradle to grave, but that's hard to do when trouble seems to lurk over your shoulder like a misshapen goblin or ghoul, cackling with madness and leading you straight into said trouble with a crooked, pointing finger.

All this, of course, would be much easier if we could see into the future; if we could see the upcoming fork in the road, one sign saying, *'Rider, this is the correct road to take. It is full of sunshine and happiness!'* and the other sign saying *'Rider, go this way and you will find trouble!'* But, as we all know, this is not how life works. And even if it did, I'd still take the road of goblin-laden trouble.

I seem to be twisted that way.

It's not that I'm particularly happy to roll down that road and into the town of Troubleville to see what madness the *Imminence* has in store for me, it's because I feel compelled; driven. I feel it is my obligation, my duty, though I do not know why.

I do not know what the *Imminence* is, or if that's even the proper name for it. I suppose some would use the words clairvoyance or telepathic, but those words sound more like scam artists that pray on the desperate and poorly educated. I call it the *Imminence* because, well, that's what it feels like in my gut; that something imminently bad is going to happen. Then the compulsion to interfere surfaces, and I take the long, lonely road to Troubleville.

To make matters even more interesting are the lights. When the *Imminence* suddenly forces its way to the front of my mind, it also provides me with a kaleidoscope of lights. Over time I have learned that these lights are a communication of sorts, from the *Imminence*. Different colors mean different things, a swirling black chrome being the most dangerous and, of course, this being the color I feel destined to follow when presented.

I am thirty four years old now and, even after twelve years of my endless-highway travel of Florida, I still remember the first time the *Imminence* came rushing to the forefront of my mind. It was 1986 and, as a six year old, and successfully coercing my parents into going out for ice cream, my father loaded my mother and I up into the old Buick and headed out to the Dairy Queen.

My father owned a 1948 Buick Roadmaster, burgundy in color with a Fireball Straight Eight under the hood. He loved that car. I loved that car. My mother strongly did not like that car. "Looks like a tank from World War Two," she commented more than once and even I had to admit, it was a beast of a machine.

Once the one hundred forty-four horses were engaged, we left our subdivision via Franklin road, which lead out to the busy and retail-infested Memorial Drive. Franklin road bypassed dozens of other neighborhoods and my father despised driving it.

There were no stop signs on Franklin, but all twelve cross-streets had them, but they were sometimes ignored, especially by young males with too much testosterone in their veins. Or just careless drivers.

In the evening, after the workday was done and weary nine-to-fivers were home dining with families, both sides of Franklin Street were lined with cars, so seeing oncoming traffic from the cross streets was difficult, especially when the sun was still up and headlights were not yet in use.

"It's like a road version of Russian Roulette," my father, Jim Reel, would comment, "or some crazy pinball machine." So he would, for the most part, slow down at intersections and look both ways before proceeding through. Just to be safe.

But this evening my mother, Janet, and my father were discussing something of importance and my father was humming down Franklin at the posted thirty-five miles an hour.

The 1948 Buick Roadmaster did not have seatbelts, either in the front or rear, but at some point the previous owner had them installed, but only in the front. Thankfully both my parents were wearing them.

I was in the back seat, laying across the vast plushness that was essentially a couch in the back of the Buick.

Then a peculiar thing happened. One moment I'm staring at the closed convertible top, debating a Peanut Butter Parfait or a

Banana Split, when my vision clouded over. The white roof suddenly became a shimmering black chrome, laced with swirls of color. I almost cried out in alarm, but curiosity quickly overcame fear.

And then the black chrome changed. It offered me a picture. A picture of a speeding car. Coming down Glendale Street. A street that crossed Franklin. It was moving fast.

And I recognized the houses it was passing, namely 5598 Glendale, my friend Brian's house. Brian's house was a block from Franklin. We were a block from Glendale. The vision showed me our paths crossing at the same time. The swirling black suddenly became red and I screamed, "Stop!"

My father's reaction was instant. A tenth of a second from accelerator to brake. A fiftieth of a second for full brake engagement and the fat Michelin whitewalls howled and barked on the warm, black asphalt.

I became airborne for just a moment before impacting the back of the front seats and crumpling to the foot wells. I and the Roadmaster came to a rest at the same time as a Chevy Monte Carlo barreled through the intersection, missing our front grill by less than three feet.

There was a shocked moment of silence as the stink of burned rubber entered the car. "You okay, son?" my father asked, craning his neck over the thick, cushioned seat. I looked up to see both my mother and father's eyes staring worriedly down at me.

"Okay," I said, pulling myself back up into the seat.

"How did you know?" my mother asked, a crook in her brow beneath well-coiffed hair.

"I – I saw it coming through the windows of the parked cars," I stammered. It was a lie, but no way was I going to tell them what I really saw; all those weird colors. And it seemed to work because they both slowly turned back to the front with a measure of relief and understanding. *"Of course you did,"* their expressions said. *"No other way."*

But that was then, this is now. Both my parents were long gone from this terrestrial world. It was only me, and my Triumph, and the endless tar-laden road.

And my road was a long one. I'd started it two years after the death of my father in Jacksonville. From there to Fort Lauderdale, then Miami and then over to Naples via Alligator Alley. From there the road took me north to Sarasota and then Tampa. Hugging the coastline the road took me around the panhandle to Pensecola, backtrack to Tallahassee, then back to Jacksonville.

Start all over again.

Sometimes I'd stop in the big cities. Or not.

Sometimes I'd take a detour and head out to Key West. Or not.

24

Florida. Big state. Land of sun and citrus and blazing summers and billions of blooms of hibiscus and bougainvillea.

One thousand, four hundred, sixty eight point nine miles. I could make the drive in two days, riding thirteen hours a day, but I never did, that would be asking too much of my derriere. I usually took a month or more to make the trip. I also used to keep track of how many times I'd made the circuitous rout, but I'd lost count in the sixties somewhere.

My current whereabouts found me close to midnight on I-275, specifically on the Sunshine Skyway, heading north into St. Petersburg. I'd been in the saddle since Miami and my hindquarters had had enough for the day. My current mission was to find a hotel, scrub the road off my hide in a hot shower, then bed down for the night.

But that was not to be.

At least not right now.

A sudden path of blackish chrome appeared on the road before me.

The ghoul on my shoulder began to cackle. I could almost see his black, gnarly finger pointing the way.

"Dang," I mumbled in my helmet.

There may as well have been a roadsign: Troubleville, Next Right.

2

I may have forgotten how many times I'd circumnavigated the state of Florida, but a little clicker in my head kept count of how many times the *Imminence* borrowed me to do its bidding.

You know those clickers? Baseball coaches use them during games to keep track of how many heaters the pitcher has hurled towards home plate. They make a very distinctive and deliberate click sound. And one just sounded in my head. The new number said 358.

I don't think on it overly though, wouldn't do any good.

So now I follow its lead, and its lead this time took me to a late night diner called Jacky Jay's just a few miles into St. Pete and off a side street. It was a wreck of a place, but in twelve years of eating road chow I'd discovered that the worse the place looked, the better the food. This place looked like it could serve a mean bowl of grits with shrimp and cheese.

I guided the Triumph into the empty lot, killed the sixty horses, heeled down the stand and dismounted. I removed my helmet and straddled it over the right-hand rear-view mirror. I shoved the keys into my right jacket pocket. I massaged my weary fanny for a moment, then raked my fingers through my wind-blown beard. It was almost to my navel, perhaps a trim was in order soon.

Taking a deep breath I looked to the front of the restaurant. The *Imminence* told me something rather nasty was going on inside and judging by the colors seeping through the windows and doors, I knew it was a robbery. I'd seen it many times before.

I also knew the robber, or robbers, would have heard me approach. A Triumph Trident is not a quiet motorcycle, at least not mine. Right about now they would be discussing what to do before I came in. Probably threatening the employees with bodily harm, instructing them to tell me that the restaurant was closing and that I would have to leave.

The wood heels on my genuine, but dirty leather Cavender's boomed on the pavement as I approached the front door. I made no secret that I was coming in. My hand grasped the door handle and I pulled. Some cheap Christmas jingle bells up in the hydraulic closure device announced my arrival.

I stepped inside.

In January of 1998 I joined the military and by the time planes flew into the World Trade Center I was a Staff Sergeant In the U.S. Army, 3rd Ranger Battalion. One month later I was in

Afghanistan. A month after that I was given my walking papers. In those almost four years, the Rangers taught me a lot of things, the most important was always being aware of your environment.

Especially in a seemingly safe, but unknown surroundings.

Before the door jingled shut behind me, I was intimately aware of everything in my environment. To my immediate right, four tables with chairs upended on their tops to facilitate floor mopping. In front of me a long counter, one third of it, to the left, dedicated to the cash register. The middle third dedicated to four bar stools for convenient counter service. The right third was the desert cooler, now empty, lights off, with condensation running down inside the curved glass.

To my immediate left a small alcove with a newspaper rack. Above the rack was a hole about four inches wide, presumably where a pay phone used to hang. Since the advent and wide acceptance of cell phones, finding a pay phone is akin to finding an extinct dinosaur. Beyond the alcove lay the main dining room; twenty more tables, chairs upended on their tops, except for the booths on the far wall.

Behind the counter a plethora of coffee machines, glassware racks, tea dispensers, juice coolers, tubs of silverware and a right frightened twenty-something young girl. Her skin was milky, making her black-dyed hair stand out as well as her eyes, which were caked with black mascara, eyeliner and eyeshadow. She had kind of a Gothic-Raccoon look going on. Add to that the giant silver nose ring and the look was complete.

She met my eyes, but didn't blink, didn't even move or say hello.

"Pardon me, ma'am, sorry to disturb you, but I seem to be lost," I said. "I'm trying to find my way back to I-275. Could you point me in the right direction?"

"I – you –," she stammered, glancing down for a flick of a second, then continued, "go out the parking lot and turn left, drive three blocks till you hit 18th, then turn right, highway is about a mile down."

While she spoke, I continued to look around. By the time she was done I had determined there were two men in the restaurant with her, and they were not here for the grits with shrimp. One was behind the counter, probably pointing a gun up at her, hence her quick glance downward. The other one was back in the kitchen, beyond the food pass-through window. I knew this because a pan hanging from a hook was still slightly swaying over the window, the result of a thrusted, angry finger at the girl, threatening her compliance. Since he was in the kitchen area where, presumably, the office and safe were, I made him out to be the leader of the two. The Top Dog, if you will.

But not for much longer. Unbeknownst to him.

There could have been more than two, but I doubted it. Thieves prefer to work alone, but occasionally they needed a wing man, someone to keep a gun on the employees. They despise working in threes because then the loot has to be drawn three ways, and they're not fond of that.

"Why, thank you young lady," I said. "Your help is appreciated. I'm much obliged." Then I turned for the door and did two things very quickly. First I pulled a toothpick from my pocket and, as I palmed the door open, I jammed the pick into the locking latch, then broke it off. The twist lock could still be turned from the inside, but the drop-hook style latch would not fall into the corresponding hole in the door frame. Second I turned back to the girl, just before the door closed and mouthed, "*I'll be back.*"

She only blinked.

I mounted my bike, but did not put my helmet on. Retrieving the keys from my pocket, I inserted the proper one and then kicked the engine over. It was still warm, so she came to life immediately. I revved the engine a couple times, just for audible show, then heeled the kickstand up. Then I dropped the engine into first, gave it some juice and drove out of the parking lot. I revved it up high, again for show, but braked about half a block down the street.

Guiding my two wheels into Bob's Carpets parking lot,

advertising free installation when you buy three rooms, I killed the engine yet again and parked. My boots made a lot of noise making my way back to Jackie Jay's, but once back in the parking lot, I walked on my toes. Not a comfortable feat for a man who stands six foot four. And I probably looked silly doing it too.

Once at the door I grabbed the handle and pulled gently. I peeked inside. The girl was gone, and there was yelling in the back kitchen area. I pulled more and once open about six inches I reached inside and up. Going by limited vision, I gently grabbed the Christmas bells and lifted them above the arc that the hydraulic arm would take, then opened the door fully and stepped inside. A fairly comfortable feat for a man who stands six foot four.

After lowering the bells, I turned and surveyed the layout again. Having been in hundreds of greasy spoons in my life, I instinctively knew there would be a aluminum, swinging door somewhere that led into and out of the kitchen, and the layout of Jacky Jay's told me that door would be to the left, around the corner from the cash register.

The yelling in the kitchen intensified. "Dammit! Just open the safe!" came a male voice.

"I don't have the combination!" Raccoon Girl responded, her voice quavering.

Still walking on my toes I quickly made my way to the

left of the cash register and confirmed my aluminum door theory. Thankfully it also had one of those windows set into it, surrounded by a thick rubber gasket. Slowly I leaned over for a quick peek, then pulled back. Two men, one big, one small, girl on her knees, her mascara running down her cheeks, the little guy pointing the gun at her, but not aiming very well.

Quickly I took two steps to my left, swatted a chair off the nearest table, then took two steps back to my right, winding up on the other, hinged side of the door. I was in place before the chair hit the floor.

"Fuck!" exclaimed one of the guys, I assumed the big one, the one who considered himself Top Dog.

For a few moments more anyway.

Then, at a whisper, he asked, "Didn't you lock the fuckin' door?"

"Yeah, yeah I locked it! It's just a chair, fell off the table!" was the reply. Then, "Look, she ain't got the combination, we got the cash from the register!"

But I knew this wasn't enough for Top Dog. I'm pretty sure he knew the girl didn't have the combination, but he was just enjoying being the Top Dog right now. Testosterone flowing, endorphins flooding his little brain, his definition of being a man.

That definition was about to change.

I knew he'd want to check on the falling chair himself. He

was the Top Dog, and Top Dog's think they're in control, that they've got it all covered, that the falling chair should answer to him for disturbing the situation.

I also knew he'd come out of the kitchen leading with the gun at full arms' length. A fool's stance, a Drill Sergeant once told me. A fully extended arm is weak, vulnerable.

Sure enough the door began to swing open. I ducked slightly to avoid being seen as the window exposed my position. First a barrel, then the trigger housing, then fingers around a grip, then a wrist.

Too easy.

In one quick movement I brought my right hand up under the barrel and trigger housing. My left hand came down in a chop directly on his wrist. I knew a round would go off in this maneuver, and it did, but harmlessly into the ceiling above. The resulting crack was deafening in the small restaurant and the stink of sulfur quickly filled my nostrils.

But the dance wasn't done.

After crashing down on his wrist, I grabbed it in a vice-like grip and pulled forward. At the same time I leaned back, lifted my left foot and put all two hundred forty pounds center mass of the door. There was no contest really. Mass, times force, times a big aluminum door, times my foot, times stupidity.

No contest.

The door immediately came off its hinges with a bang and I let the wrist go. But I still carried myself forward as the door fell inwards. Top Dog went down in a crumple, the door falling on top of him. With my forward momentum I jumped on top of the door and balanced myself as if on a surfboard, then gave it a resounding stomp.

There was no movement underneath.

While all this was going on I had flipped the confiscated gun in my hand and by the time I came to a rest, it was pointed directly at Not Top Dog.

I really hoped he would have come to his senses and just thrown his hands up. There would have been no more violence. I would have tied him up and instructed Raccoon Girl to call the police as I made my exit. But, unfortunately, Not Top Dog had been influenced by Top Dog too much. He immediately sprang backward to a food prep table and grabbed a twelve inch chef's knife.

"Really?" I asked, still balancing on the metal door turned surfboard. "A knife against a bullet? You sure you want to dance that waltz?"

Apparently he did as he made a sudden move towards Raccoon Girl, hoping to take a hostage.

He didn't make it.

Instead he made a quick exit into whatever afterlife he

believed in with a nine millimeter between the eyes. The kitchen area behind him was going to need a serious cleaning before Jacky Jay's was allowed to reopen again. If at all.

And I kind of felt bad about that. I'm a big supporter of small, family-owned businesses, and this was going to hurt their business for sure. I hoped they had insurance.

Only after Not Top Dog hit the floor did I become aware of the screaming. Raccoon Girl, still on her knees, looking up at me in horror. I ignored her as I dismounted the makeshift surfboard and flipped it off Top Dog. He was out cold. I grabbed a nearby spool of butchers twine and trussed him up like the chicken that he was. His nose was surely broken and I'm positive the lower jaw was not supposed to stick out sideways like that. But what do I know, I'm not a doctor. During the procedure he grunted as if waking up, but a quick pop with the nine millimeter butt at the base of the skull stopped that from happening.

By the time I was done Raccoon Girl was still in a fit. I knelt down beside her and she looked away. I reached a hand up and gently took her chin and raised it. "Look in my eyes," I said, and she did so through mounding tears. "Are you alright, did they hit you?" I asked. I dropped my hand and she slowly shook her head, her breathing interrupted with sobs. Continuing to hold her eyes with mine, I said, "Whatever you do, do not look to your right, understand?" She nodded. "I saw a phone out by the cashier station, you need to go there and call the police. After you make that call go outside and sit on the sidewalk. Wait for them," I instructed, then stood. "I have to go," I said, tossing what turned out to be a beat up Ruger onto the counter. A gun like that must have gone through a lot of hands out on the streets, being sold and resold dozens of times.

I looked back down at the girl.

Her bloodshot, horrified eyes looked up at me and she said "You can't just leave," she squeaked.

"Yes I can, and yes I will," I explained while turning for the gaping maw that used to have a door. "You need to call the police. Don't lie about anything. Tell it just like it is." I started to leave, then turned back and asked, "Do you serve grits with shrimp and cheese in this fine dining establishment?"

She seemed stunned at the question, as tears pulled even more mascara down her cheeks, but after a moment, she nodded.

"Mighty fine. Perhaps I'll patronize this fine Americana Dining Establishment again one day to sample your interpretation of a southern classic."

"Wait!" she barked, and I turned back once again. "What's your name?"

"Name's Rider. You can tell the police that too, they're familiar with it," I replied, then left the restaurant. I walked back down the street to Bob's Carpets. I mounted my steed and kicked over the engine. I pulled my helmet on and fastened the strap. I heeled up the kickstand and dropped the engine into first. I gave the engine some juice and let out the clutch and headed out of the parking lot.

Imminence encounter number 358 was now in the history books.

Little did I know that encounter number 359 would test me to limits that not even the Ranger's could have prepared me for.

An encounter that would also result in my death.

3

August 14, 2014

4:20 pm

North Port, Florida

I guess you could say I like my anonymity. The only address that ties me to the world belongs to Mr. Corbetti, an old family friend and neighbor. I'd stop by every time through Jacksonville, just to pay my bike insurance over the phone, or review my bank statements.

I don't own a home, or rent an apartment. Nor do I have one of those self storage lockers either. My only possessions reside in two cracked leather saddlebags.

I like living light. A habit Uncle Sam turned me on to.

I used to have a home, the one my father willed to me, before he died. I lived there for two years after his passing, but then decided I didn't want it anymore, despite being raised there since infancy. The constant maintenance on a home grew weary for me, and I really disliked mowing the yard.

If I'd had siblings I would have given it to them to squabble over, but as an only child my only alternative was to sell it, so I did. I also sold the old Roadmaster. In the end my mother was right, not only did it look like a tank, it drove like one too. And it drank gas like a thirsty elephant. Course, Detroit wasn't really concerned with fuel economy back in the day.

So I sold it all, and gave the rest away to churches and charities, thus freeing myself of the chains, and the damned lawnmower. And now I just ride and stay at hotels most nights, or at the homes of a few acquaintances I have, like Bopper, the guy who services Lady T whenever I pass through Miami.

Yeah, I call my bike Lady T, get over it.

Sometimes I'd stay with Cora, a woman whom I'd rescued from a horribly abusive husband. He was no longer of this planet, the end result of a hunting knife to the heart.

He started it, I finished it.

Cora and I were not romantic, just friends, and she allowed me to stay in her guest room whenever I was in Sarasota. Tell you the truth, I don't think she was very much interested in men anymore anyway, and I was pretty much the last one on the planet she trusted.

But every once in a while, I'd 'borrow' a home. Not sure why I did it, something to do with assuaging the anonymity bug that lives within me. After the recession of 2008, entire neighborhoods of homes across the country sat empty, including in North Port, Florida, and I'd borrow one of these abandoned homes for a night.

It was easy enough, with my KZ250L military lock picker. I borrowed it from Uncle Sam at some point, then conventionally forgot to return it. Neat little tool.

This particular early afternoon, the coming evening of which the *Imminence* encounter 359 would change my life, I decided to borrow an abandon home in Shady Acres, a completely empty cookie cutter neighborhood on the outskirts of North Port. Some big developer bought a hundred acres, built the homes and roads and planted trees and bougainvillea and boxwood hedges and a smattering of hibiscus, then went bust. Now the bank sat on it, waiting for the market to return.

Sometimes the power was still on, and sometimes not. Sometimes I'd try three or four homes till I found one with juice still in the wires. Because I hated cold showers.

The particular home I chose this time had little to do with the power being on, as even the porch light was burning, but because the *Imminence* tweaked in my peripheral vision. Nothing dangerous, nothing threatening, just something curious about this particular residence. Intrigued, I pulled into the driveway and followed it to the back of the house where the garage stood.

Oddly enough, the detached garage wasn't locked and the door made a resounding racket as I pulled it up. I usually try to keep it quiet, but as the entire neighborhood was empty, I threw caution to the wind.

The two car garage was empty except for a scattering of dead palmetto bugs under spider webs and an old trashcan full of carpet remnants, used painter's tape and a few empty beer bottles. Retrieving my bike, I rolled it into the garage and turned it around, facing back out to the driveway. For easy egress should the need arise. Then I took a quick tour of the backyard, just to get the lay of the land.

Always know your surroundings.

Then, with my trusty lockpicker, I proceeded to the back door of the home, keyed it open, brushed my boots off on the sisal door mat, and stepped inside.

The door entered into a spacious kitchen with white tile floors and granite counter tops. The counter looked like it was missing a tooth with the absence of a stove-top oven. There was a refrigerator though, empty except for two beers in the doorway; the cheap stuff that comes in twelve packs for six bucks. Stuff I wouldn't insult my taste buds with.

A room off to the left proved to be a laundry room, sans washer and drier. There were also pantry doors that exposed spacious shelves, all empty. Walking back through the kitchen I stepped out into a living room, freshly carpeted in a color I would call beige, or maybe light brown, or perhaps taupe. I don't know, I'm not a color guy. But I do know the carpet was a style called

41

Berber, named after the Berber people from North Africa.

Five long strides brought me to the front of the living room where I pulled aside the cheap, temporary curtains from a giant bay window looking out over the front yard. The yard needed a serious mowing, perhaps by one of those monsters that mowed medians out on highways. The kind that have short chains surrounding the giant blade housings to prevent rocks from pelting cars on the road.

To my right was the front door and to my left was a long wall with what appeared to have a flat screen TV bracket mounted to it, wires like black snakes hanging from a hole in the middle. Further right was a hallway that, upon investigation, revealed two empty bedrooms and a full bath. The bathroom was nice, with open shower doors in place. No need for a shower curtain. The two bedrooms and their respective walk-in closets were empty except for more wads of blue painter's tape.

Proceeding to the other end of the house I found another small bedroom, another full bath in the hallway and, at the end of the hallway, the master bedroom and bath. Same carpet in here as well, except for the bathroom, which had black and white tiles that looked like a massive checkerboard. An abandon drop cloth lay crumpled in the corner of the otherwise empty bedroom.

I started to head back for the kitchen, but stopped at the hallway bathroom. I stepped inside, flicked on the switch and looked at myself in the mirror. Definitely time for a beard trim, it'd been two months since the last one and it was already below my sternum again. Maybe a haircut too, I thought, as I looked at my helmet-molded mop. "Rider, you look like a wild man," I said to my reflected blue eyes. My mother referred to them as angel eyes, though I'm sure no angel, much less look like one.

Then something odd occurred to me. I don't know if it was the echo my voice produced that sounded off, or if it was some other subconscious tell, but I suddenly became very, very aware that I was not in the bathroom alone.

The *Imminence* remained quiet, which was odd.

The bathroom was a small one, having only one lavatory, a toilet to the left, a shower stall taking up the entire left wall and behind me an ornate brass towel bar and a linen closet behind the currently open main door.

The etched-glass shower doors were closed.

I had not checked behind them in my initial walk-through.

Strike that up as a lesson learned.

At this point I had two choices: Turn out the light, leave the house and ride away, or I could open the door and see what was what.

I sighed. Troubleville, here I come.

Turning my head slowly, I inspected the doors. "Yep, definitely a barber in my near future," I said aloud. The doors were set atop the edge of the tub making the top rail stand about seven feet off the floor. They were made of milky glass with etchings of flowers on them and were adorned with gold trim and handles. "Maybe a beard trim too," I said.

Still the *Imminence* remained quiet, which told me that whoever was there was not a threat, but I took no chances. In one quick motion I stepped the three point five feet to the doors, reached up, grabbed the right door handle and yanked to the left. At the same time I crouched down and lifted my right hand to deflect anything that came out at me.

And something did.

Suddenly I found myself with a handful of spit and fire as a girl ejected herself from the stall with astonishing ferocity. I caught her easily enough though in mid launch by the scruff of her shirt. Standing fully upright, I lifted her and pushed her back against the shower wall. Her tenacious struggles did not stop, in fact, she fought even harder. Even as big as I am, I had difficulty holding on.

Then the verbal attack started. "Want a piece of me motherfucker? Come on! I'll kick your ass all over this house!"

I wanted to answer her, tell her no, I didn't want a piece of her, that I had no desire to go ten rounds with her either. But I was momentarily speechless in the face of her doggedness.

"Big tough guy huh? Gonna beat up a girl? You fucker! I

don't have it! Let me go!" she screamed. Then she realized that her arms weren't long enough to do any damage, but that her legs were and I caught foot in the stomach.

Two choices: One, let her go or, two, pull her into a bear hug to take her feet out of the equation. I chose the latter, no way was I letting this banshee go. She'd probably go for my eyes and I'd have to hit her, and I don't hit girls.

I opt to hit guys who hit girls, those are my favorite people to hit, and I take immense pleasure in it.

So in one quick motion I pulled her towards me while spinning her around and into a bear hug. Didn't want her facing me and risking a bite to my nose. After a moment's struggle I managed to pin her arms against her chest as I turned her away from the shower stall.

"Fucker!" she raged on, "let me go! Like your girls from behind huh? You stinking asshole! Let me go! I don't have it!" She then tried head-butt me with the back of her skull, but all she hit was my chest. Her heels were doing a number on my shins though. It's amazing how much a kick to the shins hurts. Very thin, delicate skin there.

Deciding enough was enough, I quickly lowered her to the floor and laid on top of her. Two hundred forty pounds on top of maybe a buck ten got the desired result. As breathing suddenly became a grand effort, she quieted and I was able to get my first words in. "I don't want anything you have, okay? I just came in for a shower in an abandoned home, catch some shut-eye, then leave, okay? Well, I wanted to do some laundry too, but there's no washer and drier." The girl nodded, but I wasn't satisfied. "You can stay here all you want, I don't care. You can stay in the back bedroom while I shower, then I'll leave. Got it?" The girl nodded again and I unlaced my arms and quickly stood.

She did the same and fled the bathroom, then quickly returned with an accusatory finger pointed at me. "You could have suffocated me!" she exclaimed, gasping. This girl had some spunk, that's for sure. I actually raised my hands again to defend myself.

"But I didn't, and you didn't give me much choice," I replied.

Her face was hard and angry as she held her finger up for another moment before turning and leaving the room again. Again she returned quickly, this time with hands on hips. "How'd you know I was in the shower stall?" her voice echoing in the bathroom.

I turned and sat on the toilet seat and massaged my shins through dirty denim. "Dang you kick hard," was all I said.

She took another step towards me, defiant and bold. I looked up at her and appraised her for the first time. She stood about five foot five and was about as plain as you can get. Long brown hair in a ponytail, brown eyes, no makeup and other than a cord-like necklace, she wore no jewelry, not even earrings. Her face was round and, I assumed, quite simple and pretty if it wasn't contorted with anger, as it currently was. Though she was small and surely came in at only a hundred ten or fifteen pounds, she was well muscled. Perhaps a runner or swimmer, or that yoga stuff that seems to be all the rage.

Her clothing was also plain, a short sleeve button down black shirt tucked into worn but serviceable jeans. On her feet she sported pointy black leather boots with short, thick wooden heels. No wonder my shins hurt.

"You done checking me out?" she demanded with a raised voice. This girl was the definition of tenacity.

I smiled and met her eyes. "Know your enemy," I replied.

"Am I your enemy?"

I continued to rub my shins as I answered, "I don't think so, and neither am I yours. But it seems you have *someone* after you though. Someone who *is* your enemy."

She thought on this a moment, then turned a left the bathroom again. I waited and it was a full minute before she returned. "Did you see anyone when you pulled in on that loud-ass motorcycle?" she asked, this time a little less defiantly.

As I stood, I shrugged. "Couple of squirrels doing the nasty in the middle of the road a couple blocks over. Other than that, nobody."

I thought this would bring a smile, but it didn't. "Why are you here?" she asked.

"Why are *you* here," I replied.

"I'm –," she started, but stopped.

"Look," I said while pulling my beard down and to a point, "I'm not here for you, whoever you are. I just stopped in for a shower and some sleep."

"Why don't you do that at your own home?" she asked.

"I don't have a home."

"So. Homeless guy breaking into homes?" she replied, but softer now, letting down her guard.

"I'm homeless by choice, not by fortune."

"Why?"

"You ask a lot of questions."

"I've learned to be curious and cautious."

I nodded my approval. "That's a smart lesson in life."

"And you would know why?"

I sighed and dropped my hand from my rangy beard, hooked belt loops, then thought for a long moment. "You're what, twenty? Twenty-two? Too old to be a runaway and have parents looking for you. And you told me twice you don't have it, whatever *it* is. You were prepared to go down fighting like a bobcat too. Something tells me you're in the middle of something, and some not so nice people are looking for you, and the *it* thing. How am I doing so far?" She only shrugged before I continued. "And you hiding out in an abandoned home, in an abandon neighborhood says a lot. Tells me that whoever is after you is pretty good at finding people. You don't seem surprised that I'm here after all."

She was quiet for a while, then lowered her defenses completely. "I need a lift to Tampa," was all she said. It was a statement for her, but a question for me. In other words, would I take her?

"And that tells me," I said, crossing my arms, "that whatever *it* is, you do have it, and that it must be delivered to someone. Why don't you drive yourself?"

"Did you see a car outside?"

"No."

"There's your answer."

"So, how'd you get here?"

"I ran."

"From where?"

"About two miles down the road."

"What's two miles down the road?"

"My car."

I looked at her with a crooked brow.

She sighed. "It broke down."

"I see. Well, I can take a look at it –," I started to offer, but she cut me off.

"He'll have found it by now."

"Who?"

"Bock. Darien Bock."

"Sounds like a bad guy."

"You have no idea."

And then all hell broke loose.

And it would be the longest seventeen hours of my life. Or rather, the *last* seventeen hours of my life.

4

August 14, 2014

4:39 pm

North Port, Florida

I suppose I come across as a tough guy to most people, but then again, as most people I come across are bad guys, they're biased. I'm really a nice guy on the inside and on the outside I clean up pretty good, especially when I put on a suit, even though the last time that happened was at my father's funeral.

I'm basically a real simple guy. Be nice to me and I'll be nice to you. Offend or insult me I'll just smile and walk away. But if you threaten me or someone else with bodily harm, well, then we have to dance a bit together.

In the end I really don't like to hit people, but sometimes they just give me no choice. Most of the time I try to give the punk or hooligan the option of backing down, sometimes they take it, sometimes not. Most of the time they don't, which is real foolish because then I have to make them take it, and my fist hurts for the rest of the day. Which is annoying because it's painful to hold the throttle open for hours on end with a sore fist.

So as we stood there in the bathroom, the *Imminence* suddenly swarmed into my vision and told me that the two men approaching the home were neither punks nor hooligans. Punks and hooligans are easy to deal with, but these guys? They were one level up and may require a bit of effort, I might even have to hit one of them more than once.

Bands of colors swarmed around the girl, bands of blue. My own color was a deep orange. Everyone has different colors, but the one color that never changed was the black chrome that represented bad, bad things. And two bad, bad things were almost to the porch of the home we currently occupied.

I must have looked a bit spacy as I stood there letting the *Imminence* fill my mind with information. "You okay?" the girl asked.

I nodded. "The door behind you, there's a closet there. You should take cover there till this is over."

"Why?"

"We've got company."

"Who?"

"You ask a lot of questions."

She started to open her mouth again, then shut it and retreated to the closet. It was a small closet, but she was a small girl. Perfect fit.

"Don't come out until I call for you," I said as she closed

the door. The moment it snicked shut a thunderous boom came from the living room, the distinct sound of a boot kicking a door inwards. And that door not standing a chance.

I didn't move, just let the *Imminence* talk to me with colors and flashes. I have no choice in what information the *Imminence* gives me, but the greater the threat, the more it gives. And right now it was giving me plenty.

Two men were now entering the home, weapons drawn. One big guy, one little guy. The brawn and the brains, respectively. Before the big guy opened his mouth, I knew my course of action.

"You got two choices motorcycle man," his Boston accent rolled down the hallway. "Choice number one, I come find you, but I shoot first and look second. Choice number two, you come on out here with the girl and we all have a nice little group hug in this beautiful living room. Whataya say?"

Thought the *Imminence* gives me information, it does not give me a course of action. I'm dumb about a lot of things, but being able to defend myself is not one of them, a result of four years under the tutelage of Uncle Sam. So I steeled myself and walked out of the bathroom and down the hall to the living room.

No decision really, I may be pretty tough, but I can't stop a bullet. Well, I suppose I could, but the end result would be – unfortunate. Probably messy too.

It should also be known that I'm not an actor either, but I can put on a show when the time calls. And right now was one of those times. I hung my head slightly and began to wobble as if drunk. I hung my arms limply and slumped my shoulders. As I entered the living room, I did not look up, keeping as submissive a posture as I could. It wasn't an Oscar performance, but it had its desired affect.

"Oh yeah!" the big guy said. "You're a big one! Didn't look that big when we saw you ride up." His teeth were big, white, straight and square. Never punch a guy in the mouth with teeth like this, you'll just shred your fingers.

I continued to wobble as I made my way to the two men, but out of my upper peripheral vision, I examined the targets. The small guy looked vaguely similar to a rodent of some sort; pointy face, small eyes and nose. But he had keen eyes, eyes that now softened and relaxed now that he knew he was only confronting a big, hairy, drunk guy. In fact, he actually lowered his weapon.

The big guy looked more or less like an offensive tackle straight from the NFL. He was big and powerful with a block for a head, a short neck sitting atop anvils for shoulders and thick, barrel chest. I guessed the gym was his second home.

Obviously he would have to go down first.

I came to a stop about two point five feet from Offensive Tackle and three feet from Rodent Guy. Offensive Tackle still held his weapon up, aimed at the tip of my nose.

I waited for the tell.

"Fuckin' drunk are ya big boy? A little too much tequila? Ridin' a bike while drunk, that's a DWI offense if I'm not mistaken," he spouted off. A stink of too much aftershave rolled off him in waves. It was nauseating and I felt sorry for Rodent Guy having to be closed up in a car with him all day.

"Don wan no prolems," I slurred. "Just wanna a shower. Jus clean up an move on. No prolems." I continued to weave slightly and made a small stumble motion.

And waited for the tell.

Offensive Tackle smiled and leaned towards me, as confident people usually do, inserting themselves into someone's personal space. Dominating them in a sense. He opened his mouth to say something, but the words never came out.

Because the tell finally came: the weapon muzzle dropped slightly and the trigger finger loosened.

The words solar plexus is somewhat of a slang term, the proper name is the celiac plexus. It's located just below the ribcage, but just above the stomach. Perhaps right up there with the temple, it is the ultimate weak spot in the human anatomy. In this one small area the superior mesenteric artery and renal arteries branch from the abdominal aorta. Behind this area is the omental bursa, the diaphragm and on level of the first lumbar vertebra. There is also a network of fibers in the area called the celiac ganglia.

It does not matter how big the man is, or how strong he is. Punch a man bare-fisted in this exact spot and he goes down. It's the reason martial artists spend so much time building up six-pack abs. Muscle absorbs a blow to this area. It's also the reason boxers wear gloves.

Five foot six, or six foot five. One hundred fifty or three hundred fifty pounds. You hit a man in this area properly, he will go down. No question. I've even heard of people dying after being punched in the celiac plexus and though I've done it many times, none resulted in a death.

I would've felt bad about that.

I don't know why so many people aim for each others heads when they fight. The skull is thick and hard, fingers are delicate. There are much better places to punch. Nice, soft places that are much more effective.

And your hand doesn't hurt the next day.

As Offensive Tackle leaned in towards me, I leaned back slightly. But this was just a ruse. I quickly leaned back forward while raising my left arm. It easily knocked the gun out of my face and I continued to lean forward, letting the whole of my body weight fall in behind my right fist, which was on its way to a nice, soft spot.

Though it can be broken easily, the human fist is an amazing machine. The phalanges and metacarpals curl inward, backed by the carpus, backed by the powerful radius and ulna bones of the forearm, backed by the highly powerful strength of the humerus, backed by the solid foundation of the scapula and clavicle, the human fist, small as it is, can inflict serious damage to any part of the human body.

When you punch someone in the soft, spongy area of the celiac plexus, there is a bit of a recoil before your target goes backward. Your forward momentum stops and you begin to recoil yourself from the punch. In a time like this it is good to have something to offset that recoil – such as a right leg snapping up and out at chin level of someone else, such as Rodent Guy.

He never had time to raise his gun again.

In what I gauged to be right about two seconds, both of my new friends were out cold. No second punches needed.

"Dang," I said aloud, "all I wanted was a darned shower." Kneeling down, I pulled a knife from from a sheath attached to my boot then jammed it at an angle into the carpeting and pried upwards. Anyone who has owned cheap Berber carpeting knows that if one little loop gets caught in the vacuum cleaner it comes unraveled like a thread from a sock.

I pulled a bunch of threads free, cut them to length, then proceeded to tie the wrists and ankles of the fallen. "You can come out now!" I barked over my shoulder once I was completed. Returning the knife to my boot, I sat on the floor just as the girl entered the room. I half expected fear in her eyes, but she only appraised the situation calmly, nodded, then proceeded to the front door. Despite the wrecked closing mechanisms, it stayed shut just fine.

The gun from Rodent Guy had fallen to the floor, now the girl picked it up and in two quick movements dropped the magazine and ejected the round in the chamber. She inspected the weapon carefully, inserted the ejected round back into the magazine, then slammed the magazine back home. She then chambered a round, put the safety on and shoved it in the back of her waistband.

"Another one over there," I said, pointing towards Offensive Tackle guy. She retrieved the weapon and repeated the inspection routine. Always thoroughly inspect an unknown weapon, you never know if its been altered or what condition it's in.

"You okay? You look a little sick," she asked after she stowed the second handgun in the front of her pants.

Sitting on the floor, I looked up at her. "Fine," I lied. Sometimes when the *Imminence* took over my vision and mind the way it did, it left me feeling sick in much the way motion sickness does. But it passed fairly quickly. "What's your name?" I asked, stalling for time.

"Dara," the girl replied.

"By the way you handle a gun I assume someone in your family taught you?"

A nod. "My father."

I thought for a moment. "Military or police?"

She cocked her head in question. "Police. Miami-Dade."

A return nod from me. "What's his rank?"

No hesitation. "His current rank is dead." She caught and held my eyes for a long moment.

"I'm sorry," I said. "Would this Darian Bock have anything to do with that?"

"He would," she answered, crossing her arms.

I waved my hands at the two captors, both of them starting to grunt themselves out of their respective naps. "I am to assume that neither of these men are Bock, but rather annoying little minions out running around trying to chase you down?"

Another nod.

I thought for a moment. "Your dad must really have ticked this Bock guy off."

Dara did not reply; just stood, boots planted, arms crossed.

Starting to feel better, I stood and turned towards the back of the house. "Where are you going?" she asked.

"Get my saddle bags."

"Why?"

"So I can get a shower."

"A shower? Now?" she asked with an incredulous look.

I turned to look at her. "Yep. You earlier mentioned, in our little bathroom tussle, that I stink. And the danger is over, for now, so what better time?"

Dara looked dumbfounded. "What the fuck do I do with these guys?"

I turned away and headed for the back door. "Beats me," I replied. "Catch up on old times, sing lullaby's, talk about the stock market. The big guy's from Boston, ask him about the Red Sox. You know, make conversation."

A minute later I returned to the living room, saddlebags in tow, and Dara was down on her knees behind the big guy. She had the muzzle of what I saw to be a Walther PPQ shoved against his ass so hard that his pant seat was actually going up his butt crack. I stopped and said, "Interesting method of conversation, but whatever works for you."

"Fuck you," Dara barked.

"Potty mouth," I said, and headed off for the shower.

5

5:25 pm

North Port, Florida

I was in and out of the shower in less than ten minutes, I don't believe in languishing, unless it's over food. Languishing over a good meal is necessary and important in life.

The house was quiet except for occasional grunts and groans from the guys on the living room floor. I dried the water off my hide, dressed in a fresh pair of jeans, a new black t-shirt with two C's on the front, interlocked, one of them backward. I had no idea what the logo meant, I only cared that it only cost a dollar on clearance at a discount store. Then I sat on the toilet lid to pull on my socks and boots. As I laced up, Dara yelled from the other room.

"What's your name?"

"Friend's call me Rider."

A pause. "Am I your friend?"

"I don't know, you didn't greet me real nice on our first meeting."

"Rider. Obviously a nickname. What's your real name?"

"Not important."

"You're not a very good conversationalist."

"Was never my strong suit, no," I replied and stood. I grabbed the damp towel and ran it over my beard and hair again. Rangy may be my look, but I'm clean rangy.

"Where'd the nickname come from?" Dara asked.

"In the army. In Afghanistan. Guys dared me to ride a camel. I did, fell off and fractured my tailbone. Hurt like hell. Guys called me Camel Rider after that. Just Rider for short." Collecting my dirty clothes, I packed them in a mesh bag and stuffed it into my saddle bags. It would be time for a stop off at a coin laundry soon. Probably needed some quarters too. And one of those little boxes of laundry detergent.

I carried my bags out to the living room and dropped them on the floor with a *whump*. Dara still had the gun muzzle up the guy's butt. "Coco Chanel?" she asked.

"What?" I asked, turning towards her.

"Your shirt, that's the logo for Coco Chanel."

"Don't know what that is," I replied, holding my hand out for one of the weapons. She obliged, it was a Beretta Px4 Storm. Damn fine weapon.

"Chanel was a woman. Clothing and fashion. Built an empire."

"Then I'm glad I'm wearing it, showing support for

women in business." I flicked the safety off the weapon and walked over to the big guy and knelt beside him. To Dara I said, "Check their pockets, pull everything out." Then I placed the gun muzzle on Offensive Tackle's giant head. His eyes looked into mine. "You were awfully kind to give me two choices earlier, but I'm afraid I can only offer you one. Hope you don't take that as being rude, I'm not normally a rude guy. I'm going to ask a question, then I'm going to say 'go' and you start spilling. Clear? Otherwise I make a real big mess on the carpet under your head and that would be really rude to the bank, what with all that cleaning up." The guy nodded in resignation.

"Bock. Who is he? Go."

The man opened his mouth, closed it, opened it again. I pulled the hammer back. It clacked into place. "Stop!" the guy barked. "I don't know how to answer the question. Tommy and I, we don't know him personally. He calls us, tells us to do something, we do it, we find money in our accounts when we're done! We've never met him!"

"Yeah, that's pretty much the story my dad was getting from some of the guys he hauled in for questioning," Dara chimed in as she rummaged pockets.

"Your dad?" I asked, looking up at her.

She nodded. "He was onto Bock. Building some sort of case."

After thinking for a moment, I removed the muzzle from the big guy's head, stood and paced for a moment, then leaned against the busted front door and shoved the nine millimeter behind my belt buckle, after lowering the hammer and engaging the safety, of course. Saw a punk in Jacksonville do this once without engaging the safety. I'm not a surgeon, but I'm pretty sure he'll never have children. Probably can't even pee right anymore.

The air smelled of soap from my shower and I hooked my thumbs through belt loops. "Give me the story," I asked, "short and sweet."

Dara had finished rummaging. Had come up with two cell phones, two wallets, a set of car keys, coins with pocket lint stuck to them and two extra magazines, fully loaded. She sighed and sat back on her feet. "I don't know the whole story, my dad kept pretty quiet about it, but this is what I do know. About three months ago my dad responded to a call on a hostage situation. He was the first one on the scene and the guy immediately surrendered to him. The guy was terrified, begging to be arrested.

"During the interrogation the guy was inconsolable, apparently crying and repeatedly saying this Bock guy was going to find him. He wanted to be thrown in jail, in solitary confinement. Bock would find and kill him otherwise. When asked how Bock would accomplish that he said colors. He would find him with his colors, or what Bock called his *Seerlights*. Said

Bock sees lights and colors in everything and can track anyone down, anywhere."

I was tapping my fingers on my jeans, but when Dara mentioned colors and lights, I stopped. "Colors?"

The big guy on the floor spoke up. "Little Missy here's right, Bock has this weird way of knowing things. It's uncanny. He has this weird ability. He says all he has to do is close his eyes and the colors talk to him."

For the first time, Rodent Guy spoke up. "Bock'll know by now."

I looked down at him. "Know what?"

"That we failed. Again," he almost whined. "He'll kill us for sure this time."

"Again?"

"They've been after me for almost a month," Dara explained. "And Bock, from what my dad told me, is none too kind on guys who fail him. Some of the one's dad investigated wound up dead a few days later."

I remained quiet for a moment, then nodded to Dara. "Go ahead," I said.

She sighed again. "Again, I don't know a lot of the details, but the guy had a cell phone. My dad traced the calls, incoming and outgoing. Had some people brought in for questioning, traced *their* cell phone calls. Every one of them were known felons, so

65

getting warrants was easy enough. All of the phones had a common number in their memory."

"Bock," I said.

Dara nodded. "In the end he was able to get a warrant to trace Bock's number and apparently a lot of them were going to the Middle East."

"Where?"

"Iran."

"Why?"

With a shrug, she replied, "Don't know, but my dad said it was big, so big in fact he said they were going to turn over all information they had to the DoD."

"Department of Defense."

"Yeah. But they didn't."

"Why?"

"Because Bock found my dad first, and all the information. Six weeks ago. Killed him. Took all the paperwork and computers."

"Where'd this happen?"

"At his home."

Though I am familiar with computers, I'm not very good with them. I'm just not a machine kind of guy, except for the one in the garage. That kind of machine I understand. But of the few things I *did* know about computers came out as a question.

"Didn't he keep a backup of the information?"

She nodded. "That's why I have to go to Tampa."

"Why? What's in Tampa?"

"Sergeant Elroy, my uncle. Tampa Police."

"Is that where the backup is?"

Dara shook her head, then reached up to her throat. She grabbed the small brown cord that I had mistaken as a necklace. Turns out it was a lanyard and as she pulled upwards, a small flash drive popped out from under her shirt collar.

6

Looking at the flash drive, a thought suddenly occurred to me. "Why don't you just drop it off at a police station? Why take it all the way to Tampa?" But Dara was shaking her head before I could finish. She stood before answering.

"My dad figured Bock's bought off a lot of cops all over the state."

"Why?"

"Don't know, but dad thought it had something to do with whatever the thing was he figured out. Anyway, he made me promise to take it to his brother if anything ever happened. Besides that, the drive is password protected and I assume only my uncle knows what the code is."

"Why didn't you just call your uncle, tell him to come get it?" I asked.

But Dara was shaking her head again. "Dad told me not to, not to involve my uncle in any way until I delivered the flash drive to him."

I pushed away from the door and surmised, "So, at some point your dad figured out Bock was onto him as well."

Dara nodded.

"So he gave you regular backups to keep safe."

Another nod. "I stopped by his house three of four times a week after school and on my way back to my apartment."

Again, I surmised aloud. "And you found his body on the last visit." Dara nodded and looked away.

"Was it these guys?" I asked, nodding to our two silent captors. From what I was hearing about Bock, they were probably thinking more about what he was going to do to them instead of our current conversation. Certain male anatomical parts were in a hypothetical vice and the twisting of said vice was, I was guessing, in their near future.

"No, they're new recruits."

Decision time.

I raised my voice. "Hey. Big guy. You got papers?" He was still for a moment, then nodded, his five-o'clock shadow scuffing the carpet. "What for?"

"Armed robbery."

"Anyone hurt?" He shook his head. "How 'bout you little guy. Papers?"

No hesitation. He nodded. "Forgery."

"Did you steal from little old ladies? Forge their checks or something?"

He shook his head. "Contract agreements. In the construction industry."

I reached down and withdrew the knife again from my boot, then proceeded to cut our captors' hands free.

"What the hell?" Dara asked.

I ignored her question. "Collect their cell phones, leave everything else," I instructed.

"We can't just let them go!" she said while picking up the two phones.

"Yes we can," I said while replacing the knife. The two captors slowly sat up and massaged their wrists. "They're more worried about Bock than us. And I'll not have their deaths on my hands. Let 'em run and try to find their own way out."

"Hey, what about our feet?" the big guy asked.

"You're a big boy, you'll figure it out," I replied. With my right hand I grabbed Dara's left arm. With my left hand I scooped up my bags and guided both towards the back door. "Ever ridden on a motorcycle?"

"Yeah."

Fifteen minutes later Dara and I were on highway I75 northbound, a road my wheels had pulled me down countless times, by day and night. I75 south along the west coast, I95 north on the east coast, I10 through the panhandle.

Repeat.

Now, as the sun lowered in the sky to our left, a need other than a shower and a fresh set of clothes made itself known to me.

Food.

As we drew closer to Sarasota, numerous road signs announced food, gas and other necessities that resided at their respective exits. One of them caught my attention, as it always did when I was in the area. I flicked my turn signal to notify the banged up Cadillac behind me that I would be exiting momentarily.

I take pride in being a courteous motor vehicle operator.

Four minutes later I pulled into the establishment of Jackson's Sarasota Seafood and killed the engine. Jackson's was a ramshackle of a place, smelling of old fish and aged wood. I parked, dismounted, handed Dara my helmet and pulled a jungle hat from my saddle bag. I popped it into shape on my leg, then tugged it on.

"You know, a gentleman would let the lady wear the helmet," Dara commented.

"The lady doesn't need to see the road."

"Touché. What are we doing here?"

"Gotta pick something up."

"Fish?"

"Brilliant deduction, be right back."

I returned a few minutes later with a small white package and handed it to Dara. "What's this?"

"Cocaine. High grade. Don't drop it. Expensive stuff."

Dara immediately held it way from her and started to get off the bike. "Hey man, I'm not into this shit, whatever you've got going down."

"Easy, easy. We'll be done with it in less that five minutes. No biggie. Quick trip down the road and we're done. No problems."

"Drugs. At a fish store."

I shrugged. "Great cover huh?"

Dara pondered this a moment, then stuck the package into her own jacket. "Just do it quick. You don't do this shit do you?"

I straddled the bike, but didn't bother to put my helmet on. "Just a couple times a month, when the mood gets me. Gotta ease the craving every once in a while. I'm not an addict or anything." Before she could reply I kicked Lady T over and drove to the other end of the strip mall to a Waffle House parking lot.

"Hungry?" I asked Dara as I heeled the kickstand down.

Dara hopped off the bike. "I guess, what do I do with this?" she asked, removing the package from her jacket. She held it out to me like it was a poisonous snake.

I took it from her, then said, "Let's get some chow, my

gut's grumbling like a bull alligator."

We entered the restaurant and an ocean of smells; waffles, toast, greasy eggs, frying hash browns and coffee. It was one of the most wonderful smells in the world to me; the smell of my mother's kitchen when I was a child.

"Hey Rider man!" exclaimed a woman from behind the counter.

"Hey Cora," I replied with a smile. Cora of the heavy makeup, long hair in a bun and ample bosom made her way to us and gave me a kiss on the cheek.

"It's been almost two months, Rider. What've you been up to?" she asked with a genuinely warm smile.

I hooked a thumb towards Dara. "Rescuing girls from boogeymen. This is Dara, by the way. Dara, this is Cora." The two exchanged pleasantries.

"Boogeymen?" the waitress asked, "that your new calling in life?"

"Apparently. Considering business cards as we speak. Can't decide between LLC or Inc. though."

"Well, I'm sure you'll figure it out Highwayman. And I see you brought me a package. Same as usual?"

"I'd be obliged," I responded. Cora took the package and Dara and I took an orange pleather booth. I tossed my hat on the seat next to me.

"Old girlfriend?" Dara asked.

"Nope," I said while tucking my beard into my shirt. Once accomplished I made a bib of an unfolded napkin.

"How do you know her?"

I shrugged while smoothing the napkin neatly against my shirt, temporarily covering Coco's beloved logo. "Through her husband. Apparently he mistook her for a set of Ludwig drums," I explained.

Dara's figured out the reference pretty quick. "He beat her?" she asked in a whisper.

Nodding, I replied, "I tried real nice to convince him otherwise, tried to be pals and everything, but he wouldn't hear of it. Then he decided I'd be better off with a knife sticking out of me. He lost that decision."

Dara's brows rose. "You killed him?"

"Well, he didn't give me much choice did he?"

As I finished my sentence a mighty hiss came from the grill area. I didn't look, but Dara did. She watched as Skip the grill guy empty the contents of my package onto the hot iron. They danced and skittered across the surface.

"Shrimp? You said it was coke."

Shrugging again, I reached for my napkin-wrapped silverware. "Shrimp with grits and cheese is my cocain," I explained. I removed the sticky circle thing from around the napkin, unrolled it, laid the silverware out carefully to my right, then smoothed out the napkin and placed it in my lap. A moment later Cora brought me a cup of coffee in a caffeine-stained earthenware mug. She asked Dara if she wanted anything, to which she replied a glass of water would be fine.

Placing my cup of coffee in front of me, I reached for the sugar and the little creamers that look like miniature office trash cans. One third of a pack of sugar and three creamers went into the steaming cup, then I stirred it carefully so as not to slop. Once complete I licked the spoon so it wouldn't make a coffee spot on the table, then I returned it to its proper position.

Then I took a sip. Perfect. Nothing better than diner coffee. I took another long, scalding sip, then placed the cup back on the table and moved the trash far to my left, out of the way.

"If you take a cup of coffee that seriously I can't imagine the treat I'm in watching you eat," Dara quipped.

"Living in the desert for two months and eating crappy food that always has sand in it teaches you to appreciate the finer things in life, like sitting down in a plush seat and enjoying a fine meal."

Dara made a face and said, "It's a Waffle House."

"One of the finest dining establishments in America. Don't know why they don't have real table cloths, and real cloth napkins, and perhaps some classical music playing. Oh, and a maître d' would be a nice touch too."

Dara opened her mouth to say something, then thought better of it. Cora brought her a water and also a menu. No menu for me, they already knew what I wanted.

Dara poked her menu. "I'll have the number three, scrambled please. Wheat toast. Bacon, not sausage." Cora made a note on her pad, then went away.

"Do you always wear a napkin for a bib?" she asked.

"Most times, why?" I asked.

Dara gave a shrug. "Gotta admit, a guy your size wearing a bib looks – you know."

"Like?"

Another little shrug. "The word silly comes to mind."

"Being concerned what other people think about you is a big mistake in life and besides, laundry days are every two weeks, I like to keep my clothes clean for as long as possible."

Dara gave a non-committal nod just as Cora stopped by with a glass of water. Dara lifted the glass and, in three long gulps, drained a third of the cup, then returned the glass to the tabletop.

I absently sipped my coffee for a few minutes before I became aware that Dara staring at me. "What?" I asked.

She paused before responding. "Thanks for helping me back there, and for helping me get to Tampa."

I didn't reply, just took another long pull of coffee. I could feel its warmth in my belly. Dara sighed and decided to try and make conversation. "So, what do you do for a living?"

"I ride."

"Where to?"

"Next place down the road."

"And then?"

"The next place."

"After that?"

"Next place."

Dara stopped the questions and looked at me as if trying to remember the combination to a bike lock. "Got family?" she asked eventually.

"Nope." I took another sip of coffee. Half the cup empty, almost time for a reheat.

"You gotta have parents."

"I did, not anymore."

"Oh, what happened?"

Another sip. "Dad. Pancreatic cancer. Mother. Aneurysm. Died in her sleep."

"Oh, sorry."

"Not your fault."

"Brother or sisters?"

I shook my head, took another sip. Good coffee. I once

tried to back off the caffeine elixir, tried one of those coffee substitutes. Made from a roasted plant root or something. That lasted exactly one sip.

"So you just ride around on your bike?"

"You ask a lot of questions."

Dara raised and dropped her shoulders slightly. "Just curious. I've been on the run for a month, it's nice to have a conversation," she said, then pulled her ponytail over her shoulder and fiddled with the little rubber band at the tip of it.

After a moment, she tried a different tact. "What's your favorite movie?"

I decided to play along. "True Grit. Jeff Bridges version."

She nodded. "Favorite music?"

I rattled off a few. "Zepelin. B.B King. Buddy Guy. Bee Gee's."

Dara snorted. "Bee Gee's?"

I didn't reply, just took another sip. Cup only a third full and Cora shows up just in time to refill. Two more creamers and a third of the remaining sugar. Stir. Sip. Steam causing condensation in my mustache.

Dara gave up on conversation and we sat for the next few minutes quietly and listened to some country song over the speaker system. Something about a guy who was so country that his dog was named Honkytonk.

Eventually Dara pulled out her cell phone and touched the screen several times. I'd seen these newfangled smart phones, but didn't own one. I didn't even have a flip phone as I saw no need for one, though that might change if pay phones kept disappearing. Eventually she put it away and looked up at me. "I only use my phone a few minutes at a time, I think that's the way Bock's been tracking me."

I looked at her over my mug rim. "Nope."

She cocked her head sideways. "You know how he's tracking me?"

"Yep."

"How?"

"Colors."

Dara rolled her eyes. "That again?"

"Yep."

"What does that even mean. And how do you know?"

I placed my coffee cup down and to the side, then leaned back. As I watched Cora come to our table, arms laden with plates of food, I said, "Not now. Time to eat."

Cora arranged our steaming and fragrant plates of food before us with utmost care and consideration. After a brief rearranging of plates, I tucked in. A bowl of grits with shrimp and cheese at nine o'clock, plate of whole wheat toast at eleven o'clock, at two o'clock a large order of hash browns, liberally swirled with ketchup of course and at three o'clock a plate of bacon and sausage, four pieces each. At the center of my meal area, the center of the clock if you will, a plate of five scrambled eggs. My coffee sat at the noon position.

"Damn, that's a lot of food," Dara commented.

"You curse too much," I replied.

"You don't curse?"

"Nope."

"Why not?"

"It's rude."

"This, coming from a guy who just beat the hell out of two other guys?"

"Well, they were rude first."

As I ate, I thought. No better time to think than when you're eating, or showering, or on a long stretch of road from one town to another while pulling asphalt under your wheels.

It is highly impolite to assume things of other people, especially ones you don't know, but people do it anyway. I've mentioned that my physical appearance is not exactly that of a college grad in a business suit, carrying a laptop in a leather briefcase and driving a Prius. My only education came from K through twelve and the military, my briefcase is a set of saddlebags and my ride has only two wheels instead of four.

I've been called a hippie, and a mongrel, but most times I

just get crinkled foreheads and down-turned brows. Sometimes the police pull me over to ask where I'm coming from, or where I'm going to. Then they let me on about my business, especially once they learn I'm a veteran. There's a bit of brotherhood respect there.

It used to bother me, but I don't think on it overly anymore. To do so would be futile. So while I ate, I decided to make an assumption about someone, which is rare for me. The assumption was that Bock also had some sort of *Imminence* abilities. Of course I had no way of knowing this, but based on the information I had so recently been fed, I had to assume he had some sort of ability not unlike mine. I couldn't find people in hiding by using the *Imminence*, as Bock apparently could, so there were some differences.

Bottom line, I couldn't be a hundred percent positive in my assumption, yet I felt it prudent to make the assumption and risk being wrong, than not make the assumption and wind up being right.

I also made the assumption that, at some point, Bock would be calling me. Personally. He'd surely know by now that Offensive Tackle and Rodent Guy had failed. Probably sent two more goons after them. Heard their story before shooting them. Discovered their cell phones missing.

The two new goons would tell Bock the story. Big guy,

rangy beard, riding a motorcycle in the company of a young girl. Bock would want to talk. Not to bargain, but because he was curious. He'd want to know who this motorcycle man was who was interfering with his business.

Maybe I'd talk to him, maybe not. Depended on my mood when one of the two cell phones rang, or buzzed, or played music, or whatever cell phones do these days. Never understood why a phone needs to play music when it rings.

One thing was perfectly clear, however. By rescuing Dara and agreeing to take her to Tampa, I was keenly aware that I was heading not for the town of Troubleville, but the metropolis.

The New York of Troubleville, if you will.

7

7:18 pm

Sarasota, Florida

Dara finished her meal in less than ten minutes, but I was only halfway complete. Life is short, one must take pleasure and appreciate the small things that bring happiness. I do not have a home, or a car, or a wife, much less children. I don't even have a job, so my pleasures are few and far between. My motorcycle is one of them, food is another.

"You eat like a choreographer directs a dance scene in a movie," Dara commented, pushing her empty plate aside. She'd pretty much eaten like a wolf, barely coming up for air before the next bite, which I actually admired. On the few dates I'd been on in my life, the girl always nitpicked at her food. I don't care for nitpickers.

"Food is heart, food is soul, food is life. Time to talk."

"But you're still eating."

"I can talk around bites."

"About what?"

I dunked a shrimp carefully into my grits, being sure to

snag a small bit of fake orange cheese on the withdrawal. I put the entire thing in my mouth and was careful to squeeze the base of the tail to insure maximum meat extraction. The cheese burned my tongue, then I chewed and swallowed. "Well, for starters, how'd you manage to hide from Bock for over a month? He seems to find others pretty easily. Why not you?"

Dara shrugged. "Incompetence? Testing new recruits? I don't know. Sometimes I think he's just toying with me."

I nodded. "Could be, or possibly one of three other things. One, he didn't think you'd be as resourceful as you are. Two, he himself was unable to come after you. Three, he *was* able to come after you, but was unwilling to do so. Number's one and three sound implausible to me, unless he's personally afraid of you for some reason. Which leaves number two, he's unable to come after you. Is he even in the country?" I asked, then shoved some bacon into my maw. It was nice and crispy, the way it should be.

Dara seemed to think about all of this carefully, her hands fidgeting with her wrinkled napkin. After a moment, she spoke, "I don't remember my dad saying anything about whether he was in the country or not, and as far as him being afraid of me? Me? A twenty-two year old girl? Don't mean to demean my own gender, but I'm not exactly the Fabulous Moolah."

"Who?"

Dara's jaw dropped. "You don't know who Mary Ellison

was?

"Who?" I repeated, then dug up a spoonful of eggs. I had to use a spoon because they were runny, the way eggs are supposed to be.

"Never mind," she said and dropped her napkin on her empty plate. We remained quiet for a few minutes as I finished my last bites. Cora came around to collect our dirty dishes and refresh my coffee one last time.

After a long sip, I placed the mug in front of me and asked, "Cell phones?"

Dara reached into her pocket and retrieved the two confiscated devices. Slid them across the table. I looked at them for a moment. They were flip phones, not smart phones, I doubted Bock would invest in the good stuff for disposable manpower.

And by disposable I mean eventually dead, not fired one day then on unemployment the next.

"Expecting one of them to ring?" Dara asked.

"Actually, yes."

A raise of eyebrows. "Bock calling to check on his mongrels?'

"Nope, Bock calling to check on me."

"You?"

"That's what *me* means."

"Why?"

"He's curious."

"Why?"

"You ask a lot of questions."

Dara's jaw turned hard. "He killed my dad." she said.

"He did," I explained. "Now he want's you dead as well. And by association, me too."

"How? He doesn't even know who you are."

"He does now," I said and collected the two phones. I shoved them in my jacket pocket then took one last slug of coffee before I took my bib napkin off and untucked my beard. Then I stood, wrenched my wallet out, shucked out two twenties and dropped them on the table. Probably ten to twelve of it would wind up being a tip for Cora. I always believe in tipping well. I put my hat on while Dara stood. As we walked out of the restaurant I said a pleasantry to Cora, who was waiting on another table. She winked at me and said, "You be safe, Highwayman."

"How does he know who you are?" Dara asked. "We've only been together for what, two hours?"

"Colors," I said, pushing the door open. The sultry summer air rolled over us like a blanket.

"That again? You going to tell me what it means?"

"Eventually. Right now we've gotta get moving."

"Why right now?"

I stopped next to my bike and removed my hat. Shoved it

into one of the saddle bags. "Pretty sure we have trouble zeroing in on us."

"More of Bock's guys?" she asked, propping herself against the kickstand side of the bike.

"Well, it ain't Jehovah's Witnesses."

"How do you know that?"

"That it's not Jehovah's Witnesses? Pretty sure those folks are morning people, they don't like to interrupt people at dinner time. Or maybe they still only hang out at airports, I don't know."

"No. That someone is after us."

"Reasonable and educated deduction," I said, pulling both cell phones out of my pocket. I held one in each hand and looked at them. "He found your dad easily enough, finds and kills his goons easy enough, found you easily enough, at least in North Port."

"But he's never succeeded in catching me."

"With you? No, not yet, but now I think that was the plan."

"What do you mean?"

"He's been using you."

"To do what?"

"To flush me out. I think he knows who I am, but can't track me, can't find me. He knew eventually our paths would cross. The *Imminence* would have mandated it."

"The *Imminence*," Dara stated, not questioned.

"It more or less told me you were in that house, though I didn't fully understand at the time," I explained, remembering the *Imminence* peaking my interest as I pulled in front of the home.

I looked up into the sky. About ten minutes till sunset and the sky was alight with blues, pinks and reads. A breeze from the west ruffled my beard and Dara's hair. Suddenly the colors of the sky were mixed with the colors of the *Imminence*, slowly creeping into my peripheral vision. The colors weren't excited, didn't seem to be doing anything really, just floating there, pulsing between black and yellow and orange. I don't know what spurred me to do such a thing, but for the first time in my life, I asked a question of the *Imminence*. *If you're trying to tell me something, I need more than that,* I asked in my head.

And the *Imminence* responded.

Colors vanished from my vision and coalesced around the phone in my right hand. I dropped the one in my left, it hit the ground and skittered for a moment before part of the plastic casing broke off. I held the remaining one up closer to my face.

It rang.

Dara stared at me. I flipped open the phone and held it against my ear. "Hello Bock," I said. There was no emotion in my voice. "Was wondering when you'd call."

"Well," came a medium-pitched voice through the tiny

speaker, "now I have fulfilled your wonderment, motorcycle man. Also known as Rider."

"And to what do I owe the pleasure of this call," I asked. "I'm not particularly interested in any magazine or periodical purchases today. And I don't need a new credit card."

Bock issued a superficial and short bark of laughter. "You're a tough man to find Rider."

"I like it that way, gives me a sense of anonymity."

"I'm sure it does. But in answer to your question, I'm just calling to say I know who you are, to tell you that your time is coming to a close, to explain to you that our paths will eventually cross."

"So, this is a courtesy call?" I asked. The red was gone out of the sky now and purple was taking over.

Again the laugh from Bock. "If you so desire to consider this a courtesy call, then that's what it is."

"And how do you know who I am?"

"But Rider! I've been following you for years! I read the newspaper stories. The child molester in Tallahassee? The rapist in Daytona? The abusive husband in Sarasota? Thieves and drug dealers all over the state. You're a busy guy Rider!"

"I like staying busy, keeps the mind young."

Bock ignored my words. "But you're an anomaly, and I don't like anomalies. I started looking into these stories, trying to find out who this good Samaritan was. But nothing, not even the police can track you down. So my interest is peaked. How do you stay hidden for so long after committing these acts of heroism? Not even I can find you Rider, and I can find anyone, anywhere."

I had, for a long time, had the same question. I'd killed a lot of men, and beaten the hell out of many more. Surely the one's that lived had given a description of me, many times over. Big hairy guy on an old motorcycle. Gravely voice. Looked dirty but smelled like soap and shampoo. Called himself Rider. Was very polite and courteous before he beat the hell out of them.

I didn't go into hiding after each *Imminence* event, I just pulled more asphalt down the road. In my years I'd seen thousands of police cars all over the state, but none of them came after and arrested me, even though I'm sure there were dozens of APB's out there looking for me. But after a while I stopped thinking about it, it served no purpose.

"I'm not a hero," I said into the mouthpiece.

"But you are Rider! Don't you watch the news?"

"I don't watch TV."

"Surely you read the newspaper?"

"Nope, it's always full of bad news."

"Well, you're a hero, Rider. You even have a Facebook fan club where people can post pictures of possible sightings of you. You have over ten thousand fans, much to the chagrin of law enforcement. They don't like vigilantes. "

This was news to me, and the thought of being regarded as a hero by so many people made me uncomfortable. "What's a Facebook?" I asked. I'd seen many sign in hotels and restaurants in my travels saying "Find us on Facebook," but I had no idea what it was, and never asked.

Bock ignored my question. "Anyway Rider, your reputation precedes you. But the fact I can't find you disturbs me, and I can't have that."

"Why?"

"Because I'm a busy man, Rider. I've got plans, big plans and I can't risk you tumbling into them. And I think you inevitably will."

"And the girl? You used her to flush me out."

"I did. Sorry about that. I can find her anytime I want, in fact, I know she's in Sarasota right now, and I assume she's with you. So now I know where you both are. I also know she still has the flash drive, so you both have to go. Unless –," he said, then paused. "I'll make you a deal, Rider. Take the flash drive from her, right now. Take it and smash it on the ground under your boot heel. Do that and I'll leave the girl alone. She can go about her merry way, find a job, get married, have some kids."

I looked at Dara, her face now illuminated by the orange-yellow glow of parking lot lights. "That's the second time today someone's made me such a fine and courteous offer. But I'm afraid I'll have to decline."

There was a long pause on the other end of the line. "I'm coming after you, Rider."

"And I'll happily await your arrival," I said and closed the phone, then flung it to the ground with the other one. It shattered in dramatic fashion. "Time to go," I said to Dara.

"Where?" Dara asked.

Without answering, I mounted the Triumph, pulled her upright and heeled up the stand. Dara straddled the seat behind me. *Imminence* lights were still in the corners of my eyes, but I couldn't interpret what they were attempting to convey.

Before pulling on my helmet, I turned and spoke over my shoulder. "Does Bock suspect you have a destination, or does he just think you're on the run?"

"I'm not sure, why?"

"Do you think he knows about your uncle?"

Dara thought carefully for a moment. "I don't think so. He and my dad were a lot alike, but they weren't that close."

"Your dad maybe ever call him for advice on the case he was working on?"

Dara shook her head. "Not that I know of. My uncle's a beat cop, my dad was in special investigations. I don't see how my uncle could have helped. Why? What are you thinking?"

I turned my head back forward. "Bock's got to figure we have a destination now that we're together. I want to see what his next moves are going to be before we involve your uncle," I explained as I jammed the key into the ignition. "We need to go on the defensive for the night, wait for Bock to show his hand while I think."

With that I kicked over the horses, yanked on my noggin toboggan and headed out of the parking lot.

It was my mistake for taking the side exit from the lot instead of main exit that was controlled by a traffic light. The side exit spilled out to a service road that led to a stop sign and I took this rout for no other reason than it was closer.

Apparently the two guy's blocking the exit assumed correctly that I would take the easy exit as well. They stood their ground as I approached, bathed in my single headlight.

The side exit was pretty isolated from the rest of the mall and parking lot and there was a single, bright street light hanging over the three-way intersection.

I stopped the bike roughly twenty feet from the young men and I felt the bike lean slightly as Dara looked around me to see what was going on. Turning my head over my shoulder, I said, "Hop off, stand on the side of the road."

She complied, then asked, "Should I go back to the restaurant?"

Shaking my head I said, "Nah, stick around, this'll be fun."

Dara moved away and I studied the two men standing in front of me. As I did so I killed the motor, slowly put the kickstand down and dismounted.

They didn't seem to be brandishing weapons, which I thought was odd, but then they satisfied my curiosity by reaching behind their backs and each of them bringing forth a pair of nunchucks.

They began swinging them, slowly at first, then they got fancy, swinging them over their arms and shoulders, chains jangling the whole time and the sticks making whooshing sounds through the air.

"Oh good," I said while taking my helmet off, "you brought toys. I like playing with toys." After my helmet was off I re-buckled the chin strap with the intention of using it as a handle.

I watched the guys for a few moments and determined that while not amateurs, they were not experts in handling the weapons. My knowledge came from a fellow sergeant in the army, a beefy Japanese guy named Jo Lin. He regularly used nunchucks not as weapons, but as part of an exercise routine.

"They take years to master, over a decade at least," he'd explained. "Try and use them as a weapon without experience and you wind up hitting yourself more than your opponent."

Had these two men before me been older, say in their thirties, I would have had some trepidation, but these guys were easily in their early twenties. Unless they started practicing when they were ten or eleven, they didn't have the knowledge to use them effectively.

"You must be more of Bock's little puppets," I said to them. When no response came, other than more swinging of their sticks, I said, "Tell you what. I just had dinner, and a full belly makes me real happy. So happy, in fact, that I'm gonna be real nice and allow you two to walk away."

No answer, just sticks swinging.

"Now I know," I said, raising a hand for emphasis, "you're feeling real tough right now, that you think those toys give you an advantage, even over the likes of someone the size of me. But I'm promising you right now, if you don't walk away, I'm going to shove those sticks in an orifice you really don't want penetrated. Unless, you know, searing pain when you go to the bathroom for the next week is your goal."

Apparently they'd had enough of my sweet talking as they charged me at the same time. The guy to my right came at me with his chucks over his shoulder, like he was ready to serve a tennis ball. The guy to my left came at me like a baseball batter.

Simple enough. Wait till they were starting to swing, then side-stop to my left. The tennis swing only resulted in contact with the ground were I'd just been. The stick made a mighty crack as it contacted the pavement.

My sudden side step threw off the swing arc of the other guy and he tried to correct at the last second. I brought my helmet up to meet the chuck and the resulting crack sounded like a gunshot. The stick deflected harmlessly up in the air.

My right fist was already on the way as the guy tried to recover for a second swing. No time to aim for a soft spot this time and I landed a full blow right into his nose. I heard something break, and I knew it wasn't my fingers.

Momentarily stunned, I grabbed him by the scruff of his shirt and spun him towards the tennis server, who was winding up for another swing himself. Despite trying to stop the swing, all he managed to do was hit his partner on the head, who fell to the ground in a crumple at my feet. I dropped my helmet next to him.

My remaining foe wasted no time rounding up for another swing, but it was too late. I stepped over the form at my feet and easily reached up and grabbed his arm before he could bring the chuck down.

This time I did have a moment to aim for a soft spot and my right fist came up into his gut. I'm pretty sure I lifted him a good two feet off the pavement before he too crumpled to the ground, out cold like his buddy.

I looked at the two, still forms for a moment, then turned

to Dara. Her eyes were wide and we stared at one another for a long moment. "Are you okay?" she finally asked.

Nodding, I replied, "Fist is going to hurt for a few days," I said, then shook the already hurting hand for effect. "You may want to turn away for a few minutes."

I could see her about to ask why, but then her eyes grew even wider. "No!"

I bent over and picked up one of the dropped sets of nunchucks.

"Rider, no!" Dara exclaimed, taking several steps towards me.

I looked up and watched her approach. "Do I look like someone who doesn't keep a promise?"

"No, you don't," she replied, reaching up and pulling the pair of chucks from my hand. "But you can't seriously do that, you'd cause serious internal injury."

I looked down at the two still forms on the ground. "I suppose," I said.

"And besides, who knows what kind of threat Bock already had hanging over their heads? Maybe their lives were at risk if they didn't comply," she finished and tossed the nunchucks to the ground. They rolled and clattered, then came to a stop against the curb.

I grunted, then repeated, "I suppose."

Relenting, Dara and I returned to the bike, mounted up and headed out of the parking lot. But before heading back to the highway, I drove a couple blocks down the street to Harry's Harley's, open till nine. Once parked I dismounted, removed my helmet and asked Dara, "What's your favorite color?"

Shrugging, Dara replied, "Yellow, I guess. Why?"

"Be right back." I headed into the store, found what I was looking for, paid and left. Dara took the new helmet without a lot of fanfare and pulled it on.

"Thanks," she said, her voice now muffled.

"I'm a safety kind of guy."

A few minutes later we were heading up the entrance ramp back to I75 north. I told Lady T where to take us and she eagerly pulled road. I needed her to do the driving because I needed to think. A frame of mind I liked to call Ride Mind.

I felt something change, something *shift* back in the parking lot. I asked the *Imminence* a question, albeit a simple one, and it had answered. That had never happened before. I needed to think about what that meant, if there was any meaning at all. Was the *Imminence* changing? Was it growing?

Turns out I was right, in a big way. Albeit with a little help.

But first, a little road rage was coming our way.

8

9:10 pm

Sarasota, FL

I75 Northbound

Lady T was a beautiful bike. Closing in on almost two hundred thousand miles. She may be an old lady, but she can still handle the road just fine. Lot's of her parts had been replaced over the years, but replacing the parts doesn't replace the soul.

Every motorcycle has an optimum high speed. The perfect speed at which the RPM's are low, vibrations are almost non-existent and the bike almost feels as if could drive itself. Lady T's perfect speed was sixty-seven miles per hour. She settled in like a purring cougar at that speed and could happily pull tar all day long.

Bopper, real name Skip Cresh, down in Miami took good care of Lady T. I'd stop in two, three times a year for oil changes and tune ups I've had the seat replaced twice. Apparently my tucas is pretty hard on not the leather, but the foam stuff underneath.

"Your ass made of granite, Rider?" Bopper had asked.

"No, marble," I'd replied.

"Aren't they the same thing? Or close to it?"

"Don't know, I'm not a geologist."

My father bought it used in 1985, when I was five years old. It had been neglected, and it showed. Rusting tailpipe, torn seat, missing mirrors, engine problems.

He parked it in the middle of the garage and over a period of a month, took it apart. After that month the entire garage floor was covered in motorcycle parts, neatly arranged on old towels and pieces of cardboard. On the table was a small stack of grease stained papers where he had taken scrupulous notes about the disassembly. He replaced the damaged, broken or missing parts and I sat with him for hours helping him clean bearings and other things I didn't know the names of. I vividly remember one Sunday afternoon sitting on the living room floor. My father rooted on the Atlanta Falcons and I sat and polished one of the chrome wheel rims. I remember the smell of wax and my father's beer and the Sunday stew my mother was cooking in the kitchen.

Then one Saturday morning he woke me early. "It's time to put her back together, son. It's time to bring the lady to life." I remember sleepily smiling up at him, all those years ago, and knowing that nothing on planet Earth would stop me from being with my dad, putting that bike back together.

Piece by piece, part by part, bolt by bolt, Lady T took

form again under my father's strong but steady and loving hands. Being five, there wasn't much I could do, but occasionally my father would ask me to screw in a screw, or hand him a part or a tool. I would ask questions and he'd carefully answer them.

"That's the brake line, son. See? The cable attaches to the handle up there. When you squeeze the handle, it pulls the cable. And then the other end of the cable – here, see? – it pulls this mechanism and makes the brake pads close right here, making the bike stop."

As the bike got closer and closer to being complete, he always kept at least half of it under a big drop-cloth. He wanted to unveil her in grand fashion. When that day came, he let me be the one to pull the cloth off her while my mother applauded and took pictures.

She was magnificent. The gas tank was shining red with the Triumph logo in white. The chrome sparkled under the garage lights. I could smell the rubber of two new, fat black tires.

My father lifted me up and placed me on the new leather seat. I had to lean way up to grasp the handlebars and my mother took a picture. My dad had the picture developed and then gave it to me. I don't see how a little boy's face could have smiled any wider. "Always keep this picture Bixley," he'd explained. "You're only five years old now, but eventually life will dole out your fair share of hardships. When that happens, look at this picture and remember that careful persistence and hard work always pay off."

I still had the picture, yellowed and cracked now. Tucked in one of my saddle bags.

Now, almost thirty years later, Lady T pulls me through life, day after day, mile after mile. And I could reach the handlebars just fine now.

But this mile, this current mile of road, was suddenly not asphalt, but chrome. Black chrome. It had overtaken us from behind, which meant that's the direction in which the danger was coming from.

Immediately I began to brake and downshift as I pulled into the emergency lane just before the exit for SR70. Once stopped I did not kill the engine, I just left her in neutral. I did not put the kickstand down, I just held her up with two legs with boots planted in scrabble that always seems to collect in the emergency lanes of highways everywhere.

"Why'd we stop?" came Dara's muffled voice over my shoulder.

"We're being followed."

"By who?"

"Rumpelstiltskin."

"Ass."

"Potty mouth," I replied. "I need to think." As soon as I saw the highway turn to chrome, a thought had occurred to me, a thought that, if it worked, I did not want to be traveling sixty-seven miles an hour.

So I looked at the chrome river next to me, then closed my eyes. The *Imminence* was still flashing wayward colors in my peripheral vision and, in my mind, I asked: *Show me.*

And the lights responded, moving from my peripheral vision to a kaleidoscope of colors that flooded my vision. Suddenly, I was no longer straddling Lady T on the side of the darkened highway.

I was now sitting behind the wheel of a car.

It took me a moment to realize and understand. The feeling was similar to that evening as a boy, in the backseat of my father's car, when the *Imminence* actually showed a real-time picture, a 'live feed' if you will.

Now I was looking through the eyes of someone, someone driving a car. The person following us.

I could also see the soft glowing lights of the dashboard, hear the quiet hum of the air conditioner, see the pool of light that raced ahead of the hood, smelled cigar smoke.

Then the mind I occupied raised a hand and massaged his temples, momentarily blocking the lights of the dashboard and the windshield.

"What's wrong?" Came an Italian-accented voice from the passenger seat.

"Dunno, sudden headache," my guy said.

The passenger grunted, then said, *"Well, they shouldn't be too much farther ahead. Bock said an old motorcycle. Guy driving, the girl on the back."*

"How's he know that shit?"

"Said the colors told 'em."

"That shit again?"

"That and what the boys down in North Port reported."

"Dill and Tommy? What'd Bock do to 'em?"

The passenger didn't respond, but I knew that he'd shrugged. A shrug that said he didn't know, but that maybe he didn't want to know. A shrug that said maybe it wasn't good at all.

"That's some weird shit. Colors. The fuck's that shit bout anyway?"

"What Nick, you wanna me to call an' ask 'em? The Man puts a shitload of Franklin's in our pockets to do a job. Wanna me to argue about it?"

"Fuck you Scootch. The guy's a whack."

"Don I know it? What, you think I don' know it? Course he's a whack. But he puts Franklin's in the wallets, right? Always delivers."

"Yeah, yeah," my guy said. *"Guy jus' give me the boogalies."*

There's a pause of about five seconds, then the passenger

asks, *"Know what gives me the boogalies?"*

"Wassat?"

"Your old ladie's ass."

"Don' you ever get tired of that same fuckin' joke?"

"Never, Nick, never."

During the conversation I had been scanning the roadway ahead through the driver's eyes. They'd just passed University Parkway. Four miles to SR70. Four miles to a mongrel and a girl sitting on a bike on the side of the road.

The conversation continued.

" Bock say where they're headed?" asked my guy.

"North. Don' know if they's got a destination."

"Big word. 'Destination.' Learn that shit by yourself?"

"Tattooed on your ol' ladies ass."

The driver ignored the jab. *"What'f they turn off?"*

"Man said he'd call if they did."

Three miles to SR70. I looked down at the speedometer. Seventy five. Moving fast.

Time to move.

For a fearful second I didn't know how to release myself from the driver's mind, but suddenly the interior of the car vanished and I opened my eyes. The exit ramp lay ahead.

My eyes flicked to the rear-view mirror. A pair of headlights in the distance, several of them in fact. No way to determine which was our pursuers. My eyes flicked up again, looked down the exit ramp.

Decision made.

I raised my foot and tapped Lady into first and headed down the ramp. At the bottom of the ramp, a driver could make two decisions, turn left or right. The decision had to be firm due to the raised concrete triangle-shaped median that split the end of the ramp where it met SR70.

Well, I suppose the driver of a four wheel drive monster truck could change his mind, but even then it would be quite a bump.

I stayed left of the triangle, as if to turn left. I kept the clutch in, engine in first and my boots planted firmly. The night air was still and humid. Several cars and trucks zipped by east and west on SR70. A light from a nearby gas station sign flickered badly, probably a bad ballast.

A motorcycle passed us from the west, cruising easily through the intersection. A Harley Davidson. New. Chrome and paint shining. Dyna Wide Glide. Big, fat, powerful machine. The rider flicked his index finger up and I returned the gesture. The cycle-man's salute.

My eyes returned to my own rear view mirror. Headlights just now coming over the rise and down the ramp. I turned my head. "Dara?"

"Yeah?" her muffled voice replied.

"Things are about to get complicated, you need to wrap your arms around me as tight as possible." She did not hesitate and two small arms suddenly had my gut in a vice.

My eyes dropped to the rear view mirror, they were halfway down the ramp, coming fast. I looked up at the now green traffic light.

I stayed put.

My eyes flicked to the concrete median, then back to the rear view mirror. The *Imminence* flared in my vision. The colors swirled, showing the passenger of the car jacking back the slide of a handgun, then hitting the power button to lower the window.

It was going to be close.

My eyes flicked to the median again, flicked back to the mirror. I started to let the clutch out, gave Lady some gas. Then a little more clutch and a little more gas. My booted feet gripped the road and I could feel my thigh muscles holding back the horses. A little more clutch, a little more gas. Lady T now screaming to be let loose. Screaming in fury that I would hold her back like this.

"Easy girl," I whispered.

Things happening fast now. Car twenty yards away. An arm coming out of the passenger window. A gun taking bad aim from a lolling, rolling suspension. Thigh muscles burning. Lady T outraged.

When the car was ten yards away I opened the gas all the way and let the clutch out. At the same time I dropped Lady into a hard right. She unleashed her fury with burning rubber and screaming horses as we burned around the corner of the median. Once around I righted her and let off the gas. Quickly cruised to the next corner.

Even over the engine noise I heard a gunshot. I did not stop to complain about it.

At the next corner. Hard twist on the accelerator and bank hard right again. Tire looses traction. Bike spins clockwise, carrying us around the corner. Lady T eagerly laying rubber, sending blue smoke into the night air. Dara holding on for dear life.

Around the second corner, this time I didn't let off the gas but rather popped the engine into second and opened all the horses the Lady could give. Sixty horses doesn't sound like a whole lot, and for a car that would be woefully poor. But for a five hundred two pound bike, it's more than plenty, and the Lady knew how to use them.

Another gunshot as, for just a moment, we were aiming right for our pursuers' Lincoln, albeit with the concrete median between us. But that lasted only for a moment as I leaned to the left and shot back up the exit ramp. All horses were now fully engaged on the road, no more burning rubber.

As I popped into third another gunshot could be heard, a wild shot for sure; trying to aim backward from a car with brakes fully engaging at a stoplight was just a desperation shot.

We quickly reached the top of the ramp and I stopped on the point that separated the highway from the exit ramp. At that very moment a black and chrome semi blasted past, eighteen wheels screaming, showering Dara and I with gravel and a mighty blast of wind. It missed us by five feet.

"Okay?" I asked over my shoulder.

Arms loosened slightly. "Yeah," came the reply. "That was pretty intense."

"Well, I was going for intense. Going for grandiose wouldn't have cut it."

Engine back in neutral, I looked in my rear view mirror again. The Lincoln sat stopped at the traffic light, brake lights glowing in the night. I could almost see them, their necks craned backward, watching me, waiting for me to make a decision.

And I only had two choices. Two is pretty limited, but it's better than having no choice at all. Choice one, I turn right and head north on I/5. Of course then the Lincoln boys would just cross SR70 and up the entrance ramp to I75 north. That would leave us in the same situation.

Not acceptable.

Choice two, I cross the northbound lanes to the interior emergency lane and head south. Once I cleared the guardrails I could cross the grassy median to the southbound lanes. Of course the Lincoln boys would just turn left, travel fifty yards, then turn left again on the southbound ramp. Same situation again.

Not acceptable.

I had to get them to commit one way or the other. The *Imminence* lights were still dancing a bit, and I decided to try something. I closed my eyes and asked quietly, "Ideas?" After a moment, the *Imminence* gave me one, a very good one, one I should have seen myself.

I turned right, onto I75 northbound, but I stayed in the emergency lane so I could watch the Lincoln over the concrete safety barrier. I brought the Lady up to thirty miles an hour and soon arrived at the bridge itself, my wheels going *thup-thup* as we made the transition from asphalt to concrete.

The Lincoln remained motionless, but I knew they were watching me.

Then we were over the bridge, wheels once again going *thup-thup*. It was getting too difficult to watch over my shoulder now, so I said to Dara at a yell, "Watch them! When they drive through the intersection northbound, yell!"

"Okay!" she replied.

I gave a little twist to the accelerator and beefed up

110

quickly to forty miles an hour. I ticked through the gears up to four. Still in the emergency lane, we arrived quickly at the junction between the highway and the northbound entryway.

"They're coming!" Dara barked.

Perfect, I thought. I checked over my shoulder and saw the lanes were clear, so I piloted the bike across two lanes and into the interior emergency lane and brought the bike up to fifty.

"Coming fast!" Dara yelled. My eyes flicked to the right hand mirror and I strongly agreed with Dara's assessment. Lincoln engines were big and powerful. Eyes back forward as pebbles and grit spun and rang like bells through my fenders.

Not good for the chrome.

Soon the median guard rails disappeared and palm trees and scrub dominated. I looked for an opening and quickly found one.

"Now! Right now! Need to do something!" Dara yelled.

And I did. An opening in the scrub showed itself, just a few feet wide. But a few feet was all I needed as I slowed the bike, left the comfort of a solid surface and drove through the opening. Once through I gave the Lady a little gas to get up a small incline. She felt bogged down in the deep grass and sandy soil, but she pulled us through. Lady was a thoroughbred horse after all, not a pack mule.

A couple more gunshots were heard behind us. Wasted,

desperate shots. I checked northbound, saw the highway was clear and brought us up and onto the southbound lanes. Lady was happy with having hard road under her again.

I returned to SR70 and exited, turned left under the bridge and continued heading east. "Where are we going?" Dara asked, but I didn't answer, because I had no idea. The nunchuck boys and Lincoln guys found and caught up with us pretty quickly. How long before the next two guys found us? Then the next two after that? How long until one of the gunshots *didn't* go wild?

Something had to change, something had sway in our favor. And then, without me even asking, the *Imminence* pulsed in my peripheral vision and told me what to do.

I had to change Dara's colors.

9

SR70, also known as Oneco-Mayakka City Road, is like a rung on a ladder. Connected to I75 on the Gulf coast and I95 on the Atlantic coast. It swoops southeast from Bradenton for a while to Arcadia, then levels off, skirting south of Lake Placid, north of Lake Okeechobee, then up and into Fort Pierce.

We weren't going as far as Fort Pierce, either of the lakes, or even Arcadia. Nice town though, that Arcadia. Named after Arcadia Albritton. She baked a cake for a guy and he liked it so much, he named a town after her. Wonder if there'll ever be a Riderville.

I doubted it, seeing as I don't bake cakes.

Our first destination was just a few miles down the street, the side lot of a shuttered gas station. It must have been closed for a while because the sign still advertised gas for a buck and two nines. I quickly parked the Triumph and Dara hopped off. I heeled the stand down and dismounted. "Don't take your helmet

113

off," I said, and Dara lowered her hands. I turned towards her, flipped my visor up and held out my hands. "I think it's reasonably safe to say that you trust me at this point?"

Dara flipped up her own visor, looked down at my hands, then up into my eyes. With a curious brow, she asked, "What, you want a hug?"

I shook my head once. "I need you to take my hands."

"Why?"

"We need to change your colors."

She started to argue, almost asked, "That again?" But I stopped her. "We don't have time, Dara. Bock can't trace me. I don't know why. But he *can* trace you. By tracing your colors. We need to change them. Right now. I'm sure more bad people are on their way, and maybe those guys will know better how to handle a handgun."

She started to raise her hands to mine. "Will it hurt?"

"No," I lied. In fact, I really had no idea what would happen. It could hurt like hell for all I knew. But Dara took my hands. Small white hands in big, beefy catcher's mitt hands.

"Close your eyes," I instructed, and she complied.

A tingling started in my shoulders first, not painful, not unpleasant. The tingle quickly moved down my arms and was accompanied by a soft wave of orange light; my own colors. It moved past my elbow, down my forearms and into my wrists and fingers.

The orange glow intensified in our joined hands and suddenly a blue hue surrounded Dara, like an aura or a wispy, soft cloud.

Then just as suddenly, like an explosion with no force or sound, the blue aura blasted away from Dara. She didn't seem to notice, didn't even flinch. Which was good, I didn't want to be a liar on the no pain claim.

The orange surrounding our interlaced hands pulsed once, then twice and Dara was engulfed in a new color, a light red, almost pink. The new color hovered around her for a moment, then faded away, as did the orange glow from our hands.

"This is your last known position," I said, releasing her hands, "someone will be here soon to investigate. We need to go," I finished and turned towards the bike.

"Wait, that's it?"

"Yep."

Dara climbed aboard, as did I. "What was my old color?"

"A light blue."

"And my new?"

"Darker side of pink."

"Why, because I'm a girl?" she asked with a snark.

"You ask too many questions."

First destination and task complete. Second destination, a

hotel ten miles down the road. I felt the need to hole up for the night, collect my thoughts, maybe get some shut-eye. I explained this to Dara when we arrived at Lakeshore Inn, which was nowhere near a lake of any sort, and Dara agreed with my reasoning.

I got a single room that had two beds. A bit cozy for two people who didn't really know one another, but Dara didn't object. I parked Lady T behind a fence that surrounded a Dumpster, thereby shielding the bike from view of searching eyes from the road.

We found our room and I dropped my bags off. Dara had nothing to drop off, except her new helmet. From there we headed back to the front of the hotel where, surprisingly, a small diner was still open. The menu was limited, but I wasn't there to eat. Recent events dictated that a beer was in order for the evening.

Dara picked a booth and we sat across from one another for the second time in less than an hour. A waitress quickly arrived with utensils and menu's. She was slight in stature with medium length, auburn hair, no makeup and a very round belly, maybe eight months along. She also had a busted lip and a fading bruise on her forehead.

"Surprised you're still open," I commented.

She nodded, but did not make eye contact. In a frail voice she replied, "Long-haul cross-state truckers drop in all hours of the night."

That our society takes so lightly the physical abuse of women and children, or anyone really, is a mystery to me. Shoplift a pair of pants, go to jail. Beat a woman, all you get is a restraining order.

I looked at her carefully before asking, "Who hit you?"

She froze for a second longer than moment, then took her order pad from her apron pocket. Then she took a pen from behind her ear. "Nothing. I walked into the kitchen when someone else was coming out. Door hit me in the face." She tried to turn so I could not study her expression, or the physical evidence.

The explanation was a lie on her part, of course. If the door would have hit anything, it would have been her pronounced midsection. There was an uncomfortable silence for a few seconds, then the *Imminence* relayed some information to my cortex. "No rest for the weary," I mumbled.

She was close enough to me, so I reached up and gently took her arm. She seemed afraid and started to pull away, but then a serene expression came over her face. My hand began to glow a soft orange, almost imperceptible. "Who hit you?" I asked again in a quiet voice. Which was a feat because speaking quietly is not usually in my repertoire.

Almost as if in a trance, she answered, "Boyfriend."

"What's his name?"

A pause, then, "Dick."

"Humph," I said looking at Dara. Her mouth was open and she stared at my hand. "Living up to his name, sounds like." I looked back up at the girl. Her name was Karen, according to her nametag. "Where is he?" I asked, hoping that he'd be within a few miles. A quick ride over, a little chit-chat, then back to the hotel. But her answer was even better.

"Kitchen," she said, hooking her head over her shoulder. I leaned back and looked. There I could see a guy through the passover window. A real bruiser, looked like. Shaved bald, tattoos on his neck, a regular at a gym somewhere. Almost as big as me.

Almost.

"Karen," I said, looking up at her eyes, "there's a chair behind you. I want you to take a seat for a few minutes, okay? My friend Dara here's a really nice girl, she'll keep you company."

She nodded. "Okay." Then turned slowly and sat, raking strands of unruly hair behind her ear.

"Be right back," I said to Dara, who was still staring with her mouth open.

"What are you going to do?" she asked.

Standing and shrugging, I replied, "We'll start by talking about the Yankees, or maybe the Mets, then we'll see where it goes from there." Then I headed off to the kitchen, my boot heels thunking on the threadbare carpet.

Why restaurant's put carpet on the dining room floor is one of life's mysteries I've never been able to figure out. Must be a full time job keeping food cleaned out of it.

In my mind, a few minutes usually means three to four minutes, but never more than five. Turns out I lied to Karen, it took almost seven minutes of chit-chat with Dick who, in the end, came around to my persuasive efforts. I was real nice too, as I always am, but in the end, he disagreed with me and we had to dance a bit together. I was in lead, he followed.

When I returned to the table I put my hand on Karen's arm again. "Karen, I personally guarantee you that Dick will never hit you again. Ever. In fact, I also convinced him to be the world's best dad when your kid comes along." I released her arm and returned to my booth seat. "Now, what kind of beer do you have on tap?"

Karen came out of her dreamlike trance and looked at me. She recited from memory a list and I chose an IPA. Dara ordered a pink lemonade. The very near future mother walked off without another word and I turned to see Dara staring at me.

"Holy shit," she said.

"Potty mouth."

"What did you do to him? Sounded like a car crash back there."

I reached and pulled a press-board coaster in front of me so my beer glass wouldn't make water rings on the table. The coaster advertised some sort of beer from Japan. "We just had a little talk is all. Unfortunately I had to damage some pots and pans during our conversation, and I feel bad about that. Professional cookware is expensive to replace."

Dara looked at me for a moment, then asked, "What was your hand doing?"

"The *Imminence*, it was comforting her somehow."

"What does that mean?"

"I don't know."

"How did you know to touch her?"

"I don't know."

Dara seemed miffed. "How did you know how to change my colors?"

"The *Imminence* told me."

"But how did you do it?"

"I don't know."

"Is there anything you do know?"

"That I'd really like a cold beer right about now." My wish was soon rewarded with a cold, twenty-two ounce glass of deep amber beauty. I took a sniff and then a sip. Cold, hoppy and bitter, the way beer should be. After a long pull, I wiped the foam from my mustache as I placed the glass on my coaster.

"What is the *Imminence*?" Dara asked, as I knew she would eventually.

"You ask a lot of questions."

"And I'd like a lot of answers."

I opened my mouth to answer, but then a lot of clanging came from the kitchen. "Sounds like my new best friend just woke up."

Dara's eyebrows raised. "You knocked him out?"

"I didn't, a sheet pan did."

Dara just stared at me.

"I like hitting guys who hit girls. I tend to get a little carried away, but I don't apologize for it."

Dara took a swallow of her pink lemonade, placed the glass on the table. She didn't use a coaster. She repeated the question. "What is the *Imminence*?"

I sighed and took another sip of beer. "I don't know exactly. It tells me when bad things are going to happen to someone, when they're in imminent peril. And then it gives me information, sometimes a lot, sometimes a little. Then I intervene."

"What, it like talks to you inside your head?"

Shaking my head, I explained, "No, it communicates by using colors. Everything has colors, an aura if you will, even emotions have colors. I don't see them all the time, just when the

Imminence allows it, when something bad is going to happen." I went on to tell her about that day in Afghanistan, by far the worst encounter I'd ever had with the *Imminence*.

"You shot a little girl?" Dara asked, a stunned look on her face. "Why?"

"I had to, she was an imminent threat."

"How can a little girl be an imminent threat?"

I huffed. "In that area of the world? Lot's of ways. The children there are brainwashed early and repeatedly."

"That I know, but why was the girl a threat?"

I held Dara's gaze for a few moments, then dropped my eyes and fiddled with my beer glass. "It was a long time ago. A different world, a different place. Not something I care to remember, much less talk about," I said, then looked back up. Dara considered this, then acquiesced with a nod. I then gave her other examples, including the encounter at Jacky Jay's a few months prior.

Dara listened intently and said nothing until I was done. "So, you're like a vigilante?"

I strongly disliked that word. I shook my head slowly. "A vigilante is aware of his quarry and appoints himself to the task. I do not know my quarry till the very end, and I'm not self-appointed, the *Imminence* – directs me."

"So, what are you then?"

I took another tug of beer, swallowed slowly and enjoyed the bitter, herbal aftertaste, then placed it back on the round of pressed paperboard. It was starting to swell with the condensation running down the side of the glass. "I'm just a guy who rides a motorcycle."

Dara seemed to think a long moment. "And you think Bock is like you?"

"There's nobody like me, I'm one of a kind, handsome even, when I wear a suit. But I think Bock has a similar ability, though I'm just guessing."

"And he uses it to track people. Like me." It wasn't a question.

"And directs his minions."

"But now he can't, because you changed my colors."

"For now. Bock seems to be resourceful. I wouldn't say were out of danger yet."

"So, what do we do now?"

"We get some sleep. Tomorrow we take the flash drive to your uncle."

Little did I know that sleep would not come for me that night, not quality sleep anyway. That the Overseers had other plans for me. Big plans.

Also, little did I know that I had less than twelve hours of life left on this planet.

My first life anyway.

10

11:35 pm

Lakeview Inn

Sarasota, FL

Before we left the diner, I walked back to the kitchen pass-through window and stood there for a full three minutes before Dick saw me. He was leaning over the kitchen sink with wet towels and bandages and some sort of antiseptic. A first aide kit sat open nearby. Some of the towels were pretty bloody. Both eyes were puffy and he had a hard time using his left arm, but he'd managed to patch himself up pretty good. Even managed to balance a small, industrial bag of frozen French fries against his right ear, which I'm sure was swollen by now.

When he saw me looking he flinched and raised an arm in defense, even though there was a wall between us. "We're good, right?" I asked. "Your eyes are open to the way of things?"

He nodded feverishly, causing the bag of fries to fall to the floor. "Yeah, yeah. We're good," was all he said, though it sounded funny through busted lips. I let my blue eyes bore into him for a long moment, then turned and left. There was no sign of Karen.

Dara met me in the front lobby and we departed for our room. "Saying goodby to your friend?" she asked.

I didn't reply, so she asked another question. "You never said how old you were." Why do girls like to talk so much? Not that talking is a bad thing, but neither is contemplative silence.

"You never asked," I replied while keying the door open.

"So, how old?"

I took my hat off and tossed it on the generic-looking dresser, the same model I'd seen in hundreds of other hotels. "Old enough to still be alive," was my only reply.

Dara looked at me for a moment, a stern look similar to the one she gave me in the bathroom back in the North Port home. Eventually I raised my hands in resignation. "Okay, okay, ask your questions," I said and walked to the bed. Removing my jacket and tossing it over my saddle bags, I lay down, being careful to hang my dirty boot heels over the edge, then propped two pillows under my head. Dara sat on the opposite bed, pulled her boots off.

"Ow," she muttered, massaging her feet through well worn white socks.

"Ill fitting footwear now will cost you when you get older," I commented. "Hip problems, knee problems, lower back problems."

"Thanks Doctor Rider, I'll keep that in mind."

"Just a helpful tip from me to you. No charge."

She ignored my comment. "How long were you in?" she asked and stood. Rummaging through her pockets she pulled out a small wallet, a set of car keys, some folded pieces of paper and a small change purse. All these she tossed on the bed except the change purse. This she opened via the tiny zipper and pulled out a small blister pack, presumably a pain reliever of some sort.

"Almost four years," I replied as she made her way to the sink. She filled a flimsy plastic cup with tap water, popped the little pill package open and downed its contents with the water.

"Almost? You didn't finish?" she asked and returned to her bed.

"They discharged me two months early."

"Why?"

"My father. He took ill."

"Oh, right. What did you do?"

"Army. Rangers. Didn't do much of anything till nine-eleven. Went to Afghanistan for two months, then they gave me the boot." I waited for her to ask the question, but she didn't. Most people have this need to ask if I'd killed anyone once I tell them I was in Afghanistan. It's why I try to avoid the subject.

Dara's voice went soft. "At least you got to be with your

dad before – you know."

My hair rustled against the pillow case as I nodded. "We had a good six months together."

My mother passed away when I was six, my dad when I was twenty two. I have plenty of memories of my mother, despite being so young when she died, but most of them are fuzzy. I try to bring up memories of her as often as possible in an attempt to keep what memories I have from fading away entirely.

She was a slight woman, not much bigger than Dara, and sometimes I wondered how she kept the enormous amount of love she had for my father and I in such a small body. My dad was devastated when she passed, we didn't even leave the house for days afterwords, except for the funeral of course.

Eventually though, one morning my dad woke me up and instructed me to pack some clothes. When I asked why he said we were taking a trip. I complied and together we packed the saddlebags of his other motorcycle, a Honda Goldwing. We left within the hour on a two week trip that would take us from Jacksonville to Chicago to visit some family for a few days. From there we traveled to Washington D.C. and saw the sites, including the White House, Arlington Cemetery and the Smithsonian. After a week there we headed home, stopping only once to spend the night at a hotel in Charleston.

The trip, while it did little to eliminate the sadness in our hearts, did help to clear our heads, especially my dad's, but even after our return home I would on occasion hear him crying in the next room late at night.

We spoke often about that trip during his last weeks of life, him on the couch under blankets, me in a reclining chair next to him. We were in those same positions when, a few weeks later, I awoke from a late afternoon nap to find dad no longer breathing. I remember getting up and sitting next to him and taking his hand in mine.

"Thanks, dad," I remember saying.

Then, some time later, I rose, called for an ambulance, then walked over and stood before the bay window overlooking the front yard. For fifteen years my dad kept up my mother's jonquil garden, tirelessly picking weeds and keeping excess bulbs culled. On the afternoon of his death, a single jonquil had bloomed. I remember going outside and picking that single flower, then bringing it back inside and placing it in his hand. I'm sure he would have approved.

Eventually Dara spoke, breaking me out of my memories. "What'd you do afterwords, after your dad passed away?"

I actually had to think on her questions for a moment, as it wasn't a time of my life I thought of frequently. "Odd jobs, here and there. Just tried to keep myself busy. After a while I got tired of being anchored. Sold everything. Moved on."

129

"To where?"

"Next town down the road."

Dara cocked her head. "How long have you been riding around?"

I had to think on this one too. "Eleven years now, I guess. Something like that."

With widened eyes, she asked, "You've been riding your bike – for eleven years?"

"Course not. I stop for food. For sleep. Fill the tank up. Repairs to the Lady."

A long pause, then, "No job?"

"Rescuing little girls from boogeymen," I said with a nod.

"And beating up abusive guys?"

"That too."

"You seem pretty good at it."

"I take pride in my work."

Dara pulled one leg at a time up and pulled off her socks. "Haven't had my shoes off for two days, sorry if I smell."

I turned my head towards her. "I've been in the desert with a hundred fifty men who hadn't showered in two weeks. You smell like a jonquil compared to them," I finished and for the first time since I'd met her, she laughed.

"The hell's a jonquil?" she asked once her laugh faded.

"You curse too much. It's a little flower. My mother used

to grow them."

She nodded. "You never married?"

The question caught me off guard, but for just a moment. "No," I replied.

"Why not?"

"Dated in high school a bit. And in the army. Decided I wasn't very good at it," I explained, turning my eyes back to the ceiling.

Dara rolled her socks into a tight ball, took aim and arced them across the room. They fell with a quiet thump into a small trashcan. "That's kind of sad," she said.

"It is what it is," I said with a raise of a hand.

Dara thought on this for a moment, then stood, but then sat back down. I rolled my head on the pillow and looked at her, but said nothing. She searched my face with small, soft brown eyes and seemed to consider her next question carefully.

"Why did you have to shoot that little girl?" she asked with a soft, reserved voice.

I studied her in return before responding. "Why do you need to know the answer to that?"

Dara shrugged, then sandwiched her interlaced hands between her thighs. "My dad shot a few people in his career. He said it was a painful thing to live with. To take someone's life, even though in self defense, surely creates a void in life that must

131

be filled with something, anything." She shrugged again before continuing. "You've killed people, mostly bad guys, I assume, and how you deal with that, I don't know. But how do you live with killing a little girl, and why did you have to?"

I stared long and hard at her eyes before I laced my hands behind my head and looked back to the ceiling. With a sigh, I started, "In October of 2001 the U.S. Army, 3rd Ranger Battalion deployed to Afghanistan in what was called Operation Enduring Freedom. While the Northern Alliance drove the Taliban out of Kabul, my platoon was assigned watch over a small, walled compound nearby in a little town called Maidan Shar," I explained, my eyes no longer seeing the textured ceiling.

"Though it was a personal residence, Command had intell that said there was a small contingent of Taliban fighters inside that were isolated from the main force in Kabul. My platoon was assigned guard of the residence and awaited further instructions.

"We sat there for three days in the heat and sun and air so dry it made your skin crack and peel. There were thirty of us and we worked in three eight hour shifts. Eight hours on main guard, eight in backup and eight in rest, sleep if you could get it. Sleep was hard to come by in the middle of the day. The air may only be in the eighties, but the sun baked the ground and everything else heated well into the hundreds.

"It was miserable duty, especially for a Ranger. Rangers

like to be on the move, not sitting in the dirt around a walled compound day after day. But we endured by playing cards while off guard, or telling jokes, or talking about women. Some guys read books. We all choked down MRE's. Or sometimes we wouldn't talk about anything at all, sometimes there were long stretches of staring off into the sky for hours on end, thinking about nothing in particular, or everything all at once."

I paused for a moment, collecting my memories before continuing.

"On the evening of the fourth day, the main gate opened. It was a massive double-hung job about fifteen feet high, each door about ten feet wide. It was made of solid wood and must have been eight inches thick. There was a loud pop of an inner latch being thrown, then the gates opened to a three foot gap.

"Then a little girl walked out. She was a beautiful girl, perhaps seven or eight. Too young to have to wear the burqa, her dark skin and hair seemed to glow in the early twilight and she walked towards us with a big straw basket. From fifty yards away it looked like loaves of bread poking out the top.

"But the *Imminence* told me differently. Black chrome swirled around the girl in torrents. I didn't understand at first, but then I did and I yelled at my men to get behind the Hummers. They grumbled, but did as I ordered.

"I was carrying an M249 machine gun and I remember the

ammo belt clinking as I raised it in the direction of the little girl. I remember seeing her head bob up and down through the circle of the front sight.

"Both Pashto and Farsi were supposed common languages in the area and the Army gave us cheat cards on how to say certain words in either language. The only one I remember is *vaaisaw*, Farsi for 'stop'. I yelled this at her, and whatever the one was in Pashto. I even yelled stop in English, but she kept walking towards us. She was even smiling."

I paused again to collect my thoughts. It had been many years since I'd deliberately pulled these memories up, not something I cherished.

"The closer she got the more frantic the *Imminence* lights became. Bands of black chrome swirled around the girl, but then red bands began to encircle the muzzle of the weapon. I knew I had to make a decision then and there, and that decision terrified me to my soul.

"I yelled stop one more time, quickly, in all three languages, and still she did not stop. So I pulled the trigger. The rate of fire was thirteen rounds per second, and I pumped twenty six rounds into her face and I felt a part of my soul drop from my body and into the parched ground beneath my boots, never to be reclaimed."

I took a deep breath before continuing and Dara patiently

waited. "Her head exploded in a ball of red mist that blended in with the now vermillion twilight, and shell casings and links rained down around my feet like confetti."

I suddenly felt uncomfortable lying down, so I pushed myself up and dropped my feet to the floor. I raked my fingers through my beard, then just rested my hands on my knees. "When the human head suddenly just vanishes, it takes a moment for the rest of the body to understand. The girl didn't fall immediately, it just stood there in mid stride, both feet on the ground, like a living ghost not sure of which otherworld it should occupy.

"The men behind me began yelling, but I couldn't hear them very well. It was as if they were in a distant canyon, their voices mostly lost in the wind. I was more concerned with the *Imminence*. It continued to swirl around the girl in a whirlwind. I didn't understand. If she was a threat, and she was now dead, where was the treat coming from?

"But then suddenly I did know, with perfect clarity and, as the body finally succumbed to gravity, I yelled at my men to take cover. I threw myself over and backward and as I landed the little girl's body also impacted the earth. The explosion was horrifying, like standing at the intersection of a full-speed locomotive collision. I think the blast wave actually pushed me another foot along the ground. For a full fifteen seconds rock, sand, pebbles and things I don't want to think about rained down around us like a thunderstorm from hell."

I reached up and rubbed my weary eyes before continuing. "In the hasty investigation that followed it was determined that the little girl's bread basket was indeed bread on top, but they were just cover for the C-4 cakes underneath," I explained, then dropped my hand. "Such a stupid waste. That beautiful child never had a chance at life, was instead treated like property, disposable property." Looking up at Dara, I then said, "You think I'm rough on guys who beat on women, pregnant or not? You should see what I do to people who beat or abuse kids."

Dara looked at me, not really wanting to know, but asked anyway, "What?"

"One broken bone for every sign of abuse," I said, then waved a hand in the air. "Little girl with her dad over in Daytona. Couple years ago. Saw them at a grocery store. Saw the girl's face. Followed them to their home, waited till night, then knocked on the door. He was a big guy, took a lot to break his legs. And arms. Had to use a few tools."

Dara shuddered and looked away, then asked, "So what happened?"

I shrugged. "Don't know, but I'm pretty sure he couldn't wipe his own bum for a few months. Probably had to wear adult diapers. Pretty sure he peed himself a lot."

"No, in Afghanistan."

"Oh. They asked questions. Couldn't very well tell them what I really saw, so I told them I saw wires coming out of the basket. They didn't question a whole lot, I saved my platoon after all. They even gave me a Silver Star a week later. I left it in Afghanistan when they sent me on my way."

We remained quiet for a long spell, I sensed no more questions from Dara. Eventually she stood and placed a hand on my shoulder for just a moment, then walked off towards the bathroom. "I haven't bathed in two days. Hope you don't mind my indulgence."

"Not at all," I commented, knowing full well what two days without a shower felt like, or two weeks in the desert. The bathroom door closed and I stretched out fully on the bed again and glanced around the room. There was a TV on the dresser and the black screen stared back at me blankly. The remote control was bolted to the single nightstand in between the two beds. A small table and two chairs were on the other side of Dara's bed. The table held a tri-fold, laminated advertisement for a local pizza joint.

The water came on the bathroom.

I took a deep sigh, closed my eyes and thought about what should have been this evening. A hot shower at the North Port home. Maybe go back out for a pizza, extra anchovies of course. Back to the house and catch some shuteye for six or seven hours.

Hit the road in the morning to Sarasota, maybe stay at a quaint hotel on Siesta Key. Watch the pretty ladies on the beach while reading another John MacDonald novel. I had a beat up copy of *The Lonely Silver Rain* in my pack, begging to be opened. The last of MacDonalds' twenty one Travis McGee novels. He died in eighty-six, a year after finishing the series.

Good writer, that MacDonald. And that McGee is one slick dude.

I took another deep sigh and looked once more at the ceiling. My eyes closed and I let my mind wander back to Karen and Dick, if for no other reason that they were fresh in my mind. It wasn't the first time I'd had to correct a guy's way of thinking, and it surely wouldn't be the last. It was a sad situation, made even sadder that, after he healed and regained his warped ego, would go back to beating her. Probably anyway. I don't like to think in the negative, but from my experience, once an abuser, always an abuser.

Probably shouldn't have made that promise to Karen either, but I had to at least give her some hope. Even if it's just for a little while. Even if it's long enough for her child to be born. If there's anything worse than a man beating on a woman, it's a man beating on a pregnant woman. I usually give a little extra effort on those guys, have them take an unplanned nap for a while.

And I don't mind my fists hurting after those encounters.

In mid-thought, and quite suddenly my mind swam back to reality and I opened my eyes. Perhaps it was my military training, or maybe even the *Imminence* floating in the corners of my eyes, but something told me things weren't as they should be.

The hotel room was absolutely silent and the air had a dead feel to it, as if the Earth had stopped breathing for a moment. Even the running water in the bathroom had ceased.

Alarmed, I sat up, rotated and planted my feet on the matted carpet floor. "Dara?" I called out and noted the time on the cheap digital clock. It reported 12:00 in squarish, red numbers.

No answer.

I stood and called again, "Dara?"

No answer. My voice sounded dead, like I was talking into a pillow.

Making my way to the bathroom door, I knocked gently. "Dara? You alright in there?"

No answer.

I tried the doorknob and it turned. Opened it a couple inches and asked again, "Dara?"

No answer.

I could see steam in the air through the crack, but it wasn't moving. It wasn't billowing as steam has a tendency to do. With a feeling of discomfort I pushed the door all the way open and could immediately see Dara's shadowy form through the opaque shower curtain. My fears that she had perhaps fallen and knocked herself unconscious quickly faded, but now new questions entered my mind.

"Dara?" I asked again, and again there was no answer. She was just standing there, unmoving. "Dang," I muttered, knowing I had to look in the shower, for the second time today, and feeling highly uncomfortable about it.

I stepped to the right side of the curtain and, using both hands I pulled the curtain back in such a way that I would be able to see her head, but nothing else. Even then I was uncomfortable.

I'm not a pervert you know.

But my discomfort quickly vanished when I saw hundreds of needles of water pouring down on Dara's head. Problem was, like the steam, the water wasn't moving either. It was like someone had hit a pause button and left Dara frozen in time.

11

12:00 Midnight

Sarasota, Florida

I released the shower curtain and left the bathroom, pulling the door to behind me. Once back in the main room I stopped and stood very still, thinking. The numbers on the clock still said 12:00. There was, of course, only one explanation: The *Imminence*. On many occasions the *Imminence* slowed time a little, especially when the situation was dire and it needed to feed me information in a very short period of time. How it did this, I do not know, but it had never brought time to a complete standstill, not like this, and the reason for it doing so eluded me.

Crossing the room I pulled the door open and stepped outside, turned left, and headed for the front of the hotel. There was no breeze and no sound at all, not even crickets. I passed by the large, drive-through portico and stopped when I had a clear view of the road. There, two cars sat motionless in their respective lanes, headlights on, one pointing west, the other east.

There were nights in the deserts of Afghanistan that were so still and quiet and dark, it was as if the world had just stopped in its tracks, as if someone had flicked the light switch off. But I had never experienced such absolute stillness and silence as I did at that moment.

I tried to bring the *Imminence* up in my mind, tried to focus on the lights in the corner of my vision, but it did not respond. This was a bit disconcerting, but at least there was no black chrome to be seen. Which I was happy about as I'd had my fill on fist-tangos for the day.

Even though they were highly one sided situations.

Then I was suddenly aware of a flickering light causing my shadow to dance. The hotel porch lights were still on, and I cast a long shadow, almost to the street, but there was a very faint pulse causing it to dance.

I turned slowly, hands by my sides.

There, standing under the portico was a tall, statuesque woman. She wore a full length robe of sorts that was decorated with gold piping at the seams. Her short, white hair sat atop an angular and powerful face. The rest of her body was covered by the green robe, except for her delicate hands and long fingers. What I assumed were reading glasses hung over her bosom, held there by a white lanyard that encircled her neck. She exuded authority, seemed to come from her very pores. I sensed no threat from her.

"Hello, Rider," she said with a surprisingly soft and

somehow maternal voice. "The last time I saw you, you were but a few hours old."

My initial thought was perhaps she was a nurse at the hospital of my birth, but that was ridiculous. Nurses don't have bands of light circling them like giant halos.

"Hopefully you didn't see me naked," I noted, "I don't like strangers seeing me naked." She did not respond and I approached her at an easy gait, stopping about six feet from her. "Those are interesting," I said, motioning to the five thin bands of light encircling her. Each band had a small orb of light that rotated around like an electron orbiting a nucleus. They were what caused the flickering light I'd noticed.

The woman smiled with one corner of her thin lips. "In fact, you were naked. You'd kicked your blanket off, arms and legs flailing away. My, you have grown," she said.

"Just a tad, people have a tendency to do that."

The woman didn't reply, just held my gaze for a long moment before a sad look entered her eyes. "I am sorry for the loss of your parents, your mother passed too young. She was a kind woman."

"You knew her?"

With a shake of her head, the woman replied, "I knew of them, your parents. They were good people."

Nodding, I said, "I would agree. But you have me at a

distinct disadvantage. You know of me and my folks, but I have no recollection of you."

"No, you wouldn't. I only met the three of you once, at the hospital, the day you were born," the woman explained, then the sad look in her eyes was replaced with a smile. "How your mother beamed as she held you in her arms, and your father? His pride filled the room."

In the final months of my father's life, he took immense joy in talking about my mother, saying her job as a stay at home mom was much more difficult than his full time office job. Apparently my terrible two's lasted till I was four and I was quite the terror.

As this memory slipped away, I asked, "Why were you in the hospital?"

"To see you, of course."

"Why?"

But the woman ignored the question and instead said, "My name is Constance Delacroix," she said, raising and lacing her fingers just below her breast. This motion sent a ripple through the rings of light.

"That's a lot of letters. Must be time consuming signing your name, unless, you know, you just sign CD."

Again she ignored my comment. "I am an Overseer."

"An Overseer," I said, not questioned. She smiled slightly

and nodded once. We kept eye contact for a long moment, then I asked, "I suppose you're here to answer some questions I have, about the *Imminence*?" I'm a pretty smart guy most of the time, and though the question was a stab in the dark, I could figure no other reason as to who she was and why she was here.

She nodded again, "In part, yes."

"What's the other part?"

She cocked her head slightly. "The time has come for you to fulfill your destiny, Rider. You are the next Principal."

"Sounds ominous. What is a Principal?" I asked, noticing that her eyes were the same color as mine.

"A Principal is one who has complete control of the *Seerlights*, what you call the *Imminence*. Until now you have been a soldier of the *Lights*, now you must take command."

12

12:00 Midnight

Sarasota, Florida

I said nothing for a moment, letting this information sink in. A big fat file cabinet in my mind had filled with questions over the years about the *Imminence*, questions I never thought would be answered. Questions about it, about me, about why I had this gift and what my purpose was with it. All of them unanswered.

Now, it appeared, they would be, or at least some of them I hoped.

I'm not an overly reflective guy, I take what life gives me and I'm thankful to wake up north of the sod every morning. But my mind does wander sometimes, late in the day, as Lady and I pull asphalt down one road or another. Sometimes I did wonder about my destiny.

I'm not an overly philosophical guy either, but I think a lot of people mistake destiny as being a destination. I'm not so sure about that. Some famous painter guy once said that the meaning of life is to find your gift, and the purpose of life is to give it away. I think that applies to destiny as well. Find your gift, then freely help people with it. Or something like that.

So, on those late afternoons, while humming down some lost road, and I begin to feel reflective and wonder about my destiny, I just remind myself that I'm just human, and I'm trying to do the best that I can with what I have.

Even if it involves hitting a lot of people, and killing a few others.

I met Constance's eyes and decided to backtrack a bit. "What is an Overseer?" I asked, and hooked my thumbs through belt loops.

"There are four of us, and we make up what is called Overseer Hall. Our job is to oversee the five Principal's, to guide them, to train them to one day take command."

"And who watches the watchers?" I inquired.

She understood my question. "The Overseers are guided by the Governors."

"And they are?"

"We do not know, exactly. They are very secretive," Constance replied with a slightly crooked brow.

"Are they a government entity? I've no desire to work for the government again."

"They do not give us that impression."

I pursued the line of questioning no further, because a new question came to mind. A question I'd mulled a long time ago, but had since given up as unanswerable. "I've left quite a trail behind me over the years, yet I've made no attempt to hide from the law. Why have I never been caught?"

Constance smiled and blinked. "That's part of what the Overseer's do. Your victims and witnesses? We alter their memories. Mostly you are described as a vagabond, sometimes tall, sometimes short. Sometimes black, sometimes white. Sometimes with long hair and brown eyes and sometimes with a shaved head and green eyes. Your true description is never given, or the fact that you ride a motorcycle."

I stood for a moment, pondering this information. Absently I unhooked one hand and began fiddling with the lower half of my beard. I also glanced left and right. As we were standing in the middle of the portico where cars stopped to drop people off, I half expected a car to pull in at any time, but the air was still silent, not even a breeze rustled through a nearby garden.

The garden was probably nice at one time, but it was now brown and sun-baked and contained a dozen or so plants that I did not know the names of. I'm not a gardener guy after all. My only experience with the hobby was planting a hibiscus for my mother when I was sixteen. I planted it on the tenth anniversary of her death. Never planted anything else again, except for my boots on the ground.

I turned back to Constance as I rehooked my thumb. "What if I said I don't want the job? What if I said I'm tired of hitting and killing people?"

With a slight shake of her head, she replied, "It is not a choice, Rider. It is your destiny."

"What about free will?"

Constance cocked her head again. "Why would someone openly choose not to follow their destiny?

"I like to keep my options open."

She straightened her head and offered a warm smile. "You have lived an honorable life, Rider. You like helping people, you like making a difference in their lives. You are about to be given a power that will make you even more effective. It would be unlike you to turn that opportunity down."

She was right, of course. I liked helping good people. And hurting bad people. Sometimes there is collateral damage, like the little girl in Afghanistan, but sometimes those things cannot be helped. It is the way of the world, the way of life.

I always thought that if the *Imminence* had not been in my life I would have gone on to join a police force somewhere, maybe give a go at the FBI. Someplace I could serve and help people. I suppose I could have done that anyway, but after a while there would be questions about how I knew this, or that, or another thing. Or why I'd hit some guy so hard when I should have just arrested him. I like helping people, but in unconventional ways.

I'm big and hairy and scary looking, but I'm just a softy on the inside.

I asked my next question. "Why have you taken so long to tell me these things? Why not ten years ago? Or even longer?"

The woman continued smiling. "You had to prove your mettle, not only to us, but to yourself as well. You also had to mature into a grown man and accept your limited powers as a force for good. You've succeeded, and now you must take command fully."

I blinked a few times, then asked, "There are others like me?"

The tall woman nodded. "There are four others, they have already taken command."

"Where are they?"

"Not here. In other countries."

"Five is a small number to make a difference in a world of problems.

"That's because most gifted with the *Seerlights* are not given command."

"Why?"

Constance sighed. "Sometimes they fight it, so much so that it starts to drive them mad, and then we have to take the gift away. And, unfortunately, sometimes they go rogue."

At that point something clicked in my mind and I understood all too well. Suddenly all the little dots were connected.

"Bock," I said.

Constance nodded.

I reached up and rubbed my chin through thick hair. "You took the gift from others, why not Bock?"

"He became too powerful. Come," she said, reaching her arms up, "take my hands." The movement sent her rings to dancing.

"Why?" I questioned.

"We need to go."

"Where?" I asked, suddenly feeling like Dara with all the questions.

Constance replied, "To Overseer Hall."

"What about –," I started to ask, but she cut me off.

"Dara, your charge, will be fine. Come."

After a long, contemplative moment, I stepped forward and raised my own hands. Our fingers interlaced and the world exploded with blinding ferocity.

13

11:45 pm

Sandyway Motel

Bradenton, FL

Darien Bock laid back on an old, mouldering mattress. It had lumps in it from years, perhaps decades of use. Whether from traveling businessmen or horny teenagers, Bock didn't know. Nor did he care.

The bed was located in room 4B, with some peeling paint on the walls and a stained popcorn ceiling. The only light on was a flickering one, over the vanity, and a moth was endlessly battering itself against the bulb, casting flickers throughout the room.

There was a small refrigerator in the room as well, and the condenser hummed and rattled, sometimes in harmony with the flickering light, sometimes not. There was also a TV in the room, but it was on mute as Vanna turned lighted blocks of letters.

The AC was on as well but it, like the refrigerator, rattled and groaned and under the TV stand two cockroaches squabbled over a crumb of food.

But Darian Bock was oblivious to all of this. Instead he remained supine on the lumpy mattress with a basketball-sized orb of light floating over his chest. It was mostly black chrome in color, but occasionally an arc of yellow light flashed out into the room, grounding out into the walls or ceiling.

He thought about a lot of things as he lay there with his eyes closed, primarily how Dara had suddenly vanished. The only way that could happen is if Dara had walked into a massive bank vault of some sort, or was more than a quarter mile underground. He could not trace colors through high density objects.

So Bock sent Nick and Scooch to the old gas station to investigate, but Rider and Dara were gone. And there was no vault there, much less a mineshaft entryway. In the end, Bock could only conclude that Rider had somehow changed the girl's colors, which was interesting because that was something not even he could do.

A ringing cell phone brought Bock out of his trance. The black ball of light vanished as Bock reached for and brought the phone to his ear.

"The shipment is on schedule," the voice explained. *"Ten thirty a.m., slip 44D, Suncoast Marina."*

"Very well," Bock replied, "I'll have men there to retrieve it."

"Wait, you said you would be there personally, with the

payment."

"Change of plan. Something of importance has come up, something I must deal with. My men will have the payment."

"That was not our agreement."

"I am aware of that, Senator, but this issue must be dealt with, it may jeopardize your plans."

There was a long pause on the line, then, *"What is it?"*

"A man named Rider."

"And why is he a threat?"

"I believe he has abilities much like mine."

"Then just take him out like all the others, you're good at that."

Bock sighed and sat up, letting his feet fall to the floor. "It's more complicated than that, Senator. I don't know the range of his abilities, so I must tread carefully."

The Senator cleared his throat before replying. *"Well, do what you must. Is transportation ready?"*

"It is, the delivery will arrive in New York in five days," replied Bock. He then leaned forward, placing his elbows on his knees. "This is going to change the world, Senator."

"So did nine-eleven," the senator said, brushing the comment away. *"Are we assured of the highest grade?"*

"The stabilizer DIC has been integrated, the sarin gas will be stable for at least a month. The shipment has been in rout for two weeks, it should not degrade before deployment."

"Did we get our promised number?"

"One hundred rounds, encased in aluminum shells."

"Do we have enough people in New York?"

"Senator, are you questioning my planing ability?" Bock asked with a hardened voice.

"No! No, I'm – just asking to satisfy my own curiosities, that's all."

Bock took a breath. "We have more than enough Al-Qaeda sympathizers on the receiving end. They will deploy the rounds, no questions," he explained, then continued, "we also should discuss my fee, Senator. I have a lot of men to pay for their services."

"Yes, yes," the Senator responded. *"Your payment will go through at midnight, routed through the Cayman's from Switzerland. The full agreed upon amount."*

Bock nodded in the dark room. "Thank you, Senator. Now if you'll excuse me I have a couple loose ends to tie up," he said, and clicked the off button.

*　　*　　*

Bock lay back once again on the lumpy, mouldering mattress and, closing his eyes, summoned the black orb. It arose

155

from his chest and he reached his hands up to it. Little bolts of static flashed from the black surface to his fingertips.

Fifty miles away two cell phones rang in the gloom of the parked Lincoln. Due to the oppressive Florida humidity, even at night, the windows were up and the idling engine powered the air conditioning. Nick and Scooch each pulled their respective phones from their coat pockets, saw the caller number and answered in unison: "Hey, Boss." Then they looked at each other in confusion. How did he call both of them at the same time?

"Evening, boys," Bock replied, his voice smooth and relaxed.

"Wahataya wan us to do now?" Nick asked.

"Yea, Boss, just ask, we're ready to go," Scooch added.

Bock sighed over the line. *"Actually, I'm calling to tell you your services are no longer needed. It's time for us to part company on this particular endeavor."*

Nick and Scooch looked at one another, their eyes shining in the subdued light emanating from the dashboard. "Listen, Boss, sorry we messed up," Scooch explained, "but he was pretty good on that motorcycle, like a regular Evel Knievel."

"Yeah," Nick chimed in, "but you just tell us where he is, we'll get 'em this time."

"And I appreciate your dedication, but times grows short and I have to start cutting some lines. But in thanks for your

services I'll give you a few seconds to pray to whatever god you believe in, seeing as it's time to meet Him."

The eyes of both men grew wide and they dropped their phones. They turned to their respective doors, but before they could pull the handles the locks snicked down. Both men tried pulling them back up, but to no avail.

"Boss! We're sorry, Boss!" Nick yelled.

Both men became frantic, alternating between jerking on door handles and bashing at the glass with elbows.

"Boss!"

Scooch pulled his nine millimeter out and tried to use the butt to break the window, but in his panic he couldn't get a good swing.

"We won' say nuthin, Boss! Let us out!"

Nick grabbed the steering wheel and used it as leverage to slam his shoulder into the door.

"Give us a chance, Boss! We'll get 'em! Let us out!"

Scooch leaned back, brought his feet up and tried to kick out the windshield, but old Lincoln's were built like tanks.

"Boss!" Nick yelled one more time, and then both men became still, eyes peering out the front window. There, hovering a foot over the hood, was a shining black ball. Little pops of static electricity arced from the surface.

"What – what is it?" Scooch asked at a whisper, his feet

157

still up on the dashboard. There was spittle on his chin. They were both breathing hard.

Nick didn't answer, not because he didn't know, but because he didn't have time. The black orb slammed with great violence into the hood of the car and, two seconds later, the Lincoln went from a fine American automobile to a ball of fire and twisted metal.

14

12:00 Midnight

Overseer Hall

The blinding lights of the *Imminence* calmed after a moment, and I found myself on one knee. Opening my eyes revealed a polished, wooden plank floor beneath me, my hands firmly planted against it. The hotel portico and concrete drive were long gone.

"Stand, Rider, it is over," came the voice of Constance, somewhere to my right.

I looked up, then slowly stood. Before me were four, highly ornate chairs that would be better described as small thrones. They were well padded and the exposed woodwork was dark and intricately carved. They were arranged in a semicircle around an oversized coffee table, it too highly decorated.

There were two small wooden boxes on the table.

Beyond the chairs giant bookcases flanked a wide, floor to ceiling window that looked out over a pristine lake and majestic mountains beyond. The cloudless blue sky seemed to glow.

The air smelled of wood polish, old paper and, faintly,

pipe smoke.

Three of the chairs were occupied. Constance, her circles of light now gone, made her way to the remaining empty one and sat in a regal fashion. From my left to right, she introduced the three men as Dean, Alastair and Dayton.

They were very old men, easily into their nineties, if not older. Constance was easily the younger, perhaps in her sixties. All of them had eyes that reflected wisdom and full mental faculties.

They stared at me for a long moment before I said, "It is – nice to meet you." Because I had no idea what else to say. As I've made it clear, I am not a master of conversation.

"There is a chair behind you, if you wish to sit," Dean offered. I politely declined.

"When was the last time you shaved?" Dayton asked. His eyes, surrounded by brown, leathery skin, held a look of disapproval.

"I – perhaps eight years ago," I replied. Feeling uncomfortable with my hands just hanging by my side, I hooked belt loops. After more silence I asked, "Where are we?"

This time Alastair spoke. "Wicklow Mountains, in Ireland. Beautiful, isn't it?" he asked looking over his shoulder and out the window. His wispy white hair, what was left of it, shifted with the motion.

"I don't suppose I got any frequent flier miles for the trip," was my reply and Dean chuckled. I thought to ask how I managed to go from being Florida to the mountains of Ireland, but I thought better of it. The answer surely would involve physics and I'm not a science guy.

"You look like a hippie," Dayton commented. It was obvious he was the grumpy one of the group. I did not respond to the comment.

Instead, I asked, "Why am I here?"

Dean motioned to the two boxes on the table with a frail hand adorned with rings. "Those are now yours," he explained, "you have earned them."

I looked down at the boxes. They, like the chairs and table, were of dark, carved wood. "What are they?" I asked, looking back up. I stayed standing where I was.

The *Imminence* remained quiet, not even colors in my peripheral.

Constance answered my question. "They are – shall we say – the tools of your newly acquired office, of your new command."

Again I looked at the boxes, then made two steps to the table. It was taller than a typical coffee table, but I still had to stoop. I flipped the lids up on the two boxes using little brass rings, then gazed inside.

Nested in soft fabric, two glowing balls resided. The white light wasn't overly blinding, but I still had to squint a bit. They were similar to the glowing orbs on Constance's rings, perhaps a little larger than a golf balls. I stood erect and asked again, "What are they?" I asked again.

"They are called Seer Orbs," Dayton explained, his grumpiness edging off.

"What do they do?"

"They will – enhance your abilities, as well as give you a weapon."

I held Dayton's eyes for a moment, then raised my hands and made fists. "I have weapons."

For the first time, Dayton smiled, sort of. "Yes, but with these you won't need to damage doors, or restaurant equipment."

This, obviously, interested me as I greatly disliked property damage. "How do I use them?" I asked, dropping my hands to my sides.

Dayton lifted a hand to explain, then stopped. "Pick them up, Motorcycle Man. You'll have all your answers then."

I looked back down at the glowing orbs. They just sat there, glowing and pulsing and the light seemed to have depth somehow, as if I stared into it long enough I'd get lost in them.

I fear nothing in life, but I do have a healthy trepidation about some things, heights being one of them, which the army cured me of for the most part. Nothing like jumping out of an airplane at fifteen thousand feet to cure one's fear of heights. Another fear is squirrels, specifically their evil little hands. I don't know why.

Though I did not fear the orbs before me, I had some trepidation. And the best way to defeat either is to take it to task, to face it head on, so I reached down and gently plucked the orbs into my hands. Then I pulled myself erect and simply looked at them.

They weighed close to nothing and were surprisingly warm as they settled into my cupped palms, but other than shine a bit more brightly, nothing happened. I looked up at Constance.

"Give it a moment," she said with a wry smile. "You should also consider sitting down. You're a big man and big men fall hard."

I looked at the other three men. They were all grinning. "Is this some sort of –," I started, but stopped. Because my hands suddenly felt as if they were afire. I looked down to find white light encasing my hands. I wanted to drop the orbs, wanted to make it stop, but I could not move my arms as the light quickly moved up them towards my shoulder. The pain of fire moved with it and I tried to gasp for air.

"Here we go!" Dayton said, almost gleefully.

Once the light reached my shoulders it spread out across

my chest, moved towards my waist and then my legs and feet. My head was last and I stretched my neck upwards as a drowning man might do, fighting for that last breath before being pulled under forever.

I think I hollered in pain as the light finally consumed me, and I felt myself fall to my knees. I tried to breathe, but felt I was getting no air. I tried to move, to push myself away, but I could not make my arms or legs work. Tried to will the pain away, will it away from eating at my flesh and bone. It was relentless, like a million needles pushing into my body all at once. Like a million bee stings. Like a million ice picks.

Then there was a light, inside my head, and it was blinding, as if I had no eyelids and was being forced to look into a sun. I tried to look away, but the light was everywhere, boring into my mind.

Somehow I gathered a voice in my head, then gathered a breath and yelled, "*Stop!*" And, mercifully, it did stop. The needles and stings rapidly faded. The light dimmed to darkness

As cognition began to collect itself in my mind, I became aware of a intermittent whooshing sound, very fast and deep. It took a long moment to recognize it was me, gasping for air. Felt a thundering inside me, crashing against my ribs. Another moment to realize it was my heart. Tried to open my eyes, they refused. Tried to stand, legs said no. Tried to slow and control my breathing.

At least that worked.

I do not like feeling vulnerable. Vulnerability incites panic. Panic incites poor decision making. So I controlled my breathing, slowed it down. My heart followed along, from thundering, down to hammering, down to thumping, then down to regular beating.

I breathed in slow, exhaled slower.

And then the *Imminence* returned in the eyes of my mind. But not the flashing, swooping lights I'd known all my life. They now seemed to take on an extra dimension, an extra depth. Long, flowing, almost misty contrails accompanied the lights as they swirled and danced. The choreography was almost soothing in a way, further helping my breathing and heartbeat to slow.

Then the voice of Dayton said, "It's over, hippie. You can get up."

I opened my eyes and found I was still on toes and knees, my empty, open hands laying across my thighs, the orbs no longer there. I was also slouched at the waist, causing my beard to fall over my belt buckle. I leaned to one side and brought the opposite leg from under me and planted my boot. Then I planted a hand on that knee and pushed myself erect.

It took longer than a few moments.

Then I looked up. The four Overseers still sat, and just

watched. "That was – most unpleasant," I said, still panting somewhat.

Alastair spoke up. "Yes, sorry about that. Integration, as we call it, can be – shall we say – distressing?"

I wiped sweating hands on my jeans. "That's a good adjective as well."

"What was worse?" Dayton asked with a smile, "the needles or the blinding light?"

I didn't answer, because his question brought something to light. "What, all of you have done this too?" Constance and Alastair nodded. "Then why am I here? Why don't the four of you go after people like Bock?"

Dean answered, pulling his silver-rimmed glasses to the tip of his nose. He looked at me over their rims. "Rider," he started with a smile, "we're not exactly of the age to be romping through the streets tracking down bad guys, much less fighting them. All four of us had our time doing that. Then we got old." He paused with a sigh and a look of distance on his face. "See these hands?" he asked, holding up the two frail and wrinkled appendages. I nodded and he continued. "Was a time I could take on anybody, even someone the size of you. Lay them down for the count." For emphasis he balled a fist and made a weak punch in the air, then lowered his hands to his lap, a sign of resignation in his eyes. "But those days are over, for us. And so we must pass the torch on."

I looked at Constance. "You too?"

A wry smile crept to her lips again and her eyes narrowed. "I could've taken you down in less than five seconds," she said with an almost evil purr.

I smiled. "Martial arts?"

"Eight different types."

I looked down at my own hands. Not so old. Hard, square and calloused. Already done their fair share of laying guys out. One of them less than an hour ago.

I was about to ask what happened to the little orbs of light, but as I looked at my hands, a new bit of information arose in my mind, almost as if a new owner's manual opened itself to me. I said a command in my head, and the two balls of light reappeared straight from the flesh of my hands, and hovered above my palms. They rotated slightly, little flickers of static popping and arcing.

There was no pain.

"Interesting," I stated.

"You have accepted command, Motorcycle Man," Dayton announced, "but just be aware, a bullet can still kill you, you are not immortal. Also take note of the one thing you should never, ever do with the orbs. To do so will cost you your life."

Nodding in understanding, and still looking at the orbs, I said, "Noted."

"You now have the full power of the *Seerlights*, Rider, as well as the knowledge of how to use it." This was from Alastair. "Your destiny now continues."

15

12:00 Midnight

Sarasota, Florida

Again Constance took my hands and again the world exploded in light, but not before Dayton hollered, "And get a haircut!" But when the light faded, it was only a haggard motorcycle rider standing beneath the portico.

I glanced around, but all was exactly as before we'd left. No sounds, no breeze, nothing. As my eyes moved back towards the front of the hotel, I saw something I'd not seen earlier, because Constance had blocked my view. Behind the reception desk stood a middle aged woman with a small stack of pamphlets in her hands, in the process of slipping them into a plastic holder on the counter. She was completely motionless.

With three clunks of boot heels, I turned a one-eighty and faced the hotel exit and the road beyond where the two cars still sat, frozen in time. I took a deep breath. Closed my eyes. Then let the new information open in my mind and cascade through my cortex.

In the end, there was not a lot of information. It was less

of a how-to manual and more of a dictation of capabilities. It is a strange feeling to suddenly *know* things without them having ever passed through one or more of the five senses. But know them I did, and a whole new world of possibilities lay before me. Not to mention some seriously bad days ahead for not-so-nice guys.

Of course I say this not knowing my life would end in less than ten hours.

Lifting my hands, I summoned the orbs and they arose from my palms, their flickering light dancing in the night air. Stepping to the nearest pillar holding the portico roof up, I placed my palms against the aged, red bricks and the orbs melted into their surface.

Soft pulses of light emanated down the narrow brick column and faded into the ground and immediately I could hear the harmony of humanity open up to me. Thousands upon thousands of voices culminating into a shrill static, like thousands of guitar strings being plucked at the same time.

It was then that I realized time had not stopped, that it kept lumbering on. Ever forward, never ending. Instead, it was I who had stopped, as if I'd been pulled out of time, but I didn't think on it overly, I don't understand that multi-dimential stuff.

Focusing on a few hundred of the voices, I quickly realized that most of them were in accord, but some of them were not, some of them were out of tune. Black chrome accompanied their voices.

As I stood there, with my palms on the warm bricks and my eyes closed, I focused on a few of the voices, one at a time. The first one I chose enabled me to hear and see an exhausted man in a rocking chair at a home just a few blocks away, quietly humming a song to a fussy infant in his arms. He rocked gently, patiently in the subdued light, a new crib next to him, adorned with flowery sheets and stuffed animals.

Letting that image go, I located another, about a mile away to the south. An older couple, well into their seventies, sitting close, her head on his shoulder, a blanket over their legs. The only light in the room came from a TV, playing an old black and white rerun of something, probably a movie from their past they'd both enjoyed, judging by the smiles on their faces. "Fred and Ginger were so wonderful," she was saying. "Remember seeing this in New York?" he asked in response. She nodded against his flannel robe and smiled warmly.

Uncomfortable with the eavesdropping, I let that image go as well and drew up a new rule in my head: Focus only on the voices out of tune, the voices with black chrome. Though it was nice, for a change, to experience a moment of human goodness, it is not my place. My place is Troubleville, and now it appears I've been given a new tool to get me there. A Troubleville Train, if you will.

So I focused on a voice out of tune, a note riding against the harmony.

There, behind a strip mall four miles away. A young man taking trash out from a now-closed auto part shop. He dragged a can full of plastic wrappings with one hand while cradling under his other arm flattened cardboard for the recycle bin. He dumped the cardboard first, then slammed the lid closed. He then upended the can into another bin that reeked of soured food from the fast food joint next door.

He never got a chance to close the lid because a man with a gun stepped from behind the bin and pointed the weapon at him in the poorly lit backlot. "Here's what's gonna happen," the gun-wielder said. He held the gun sideways like a gangster, like he thought it made him look cool, like he thought it made him a better man, like it made him look like a Top Dog.

Under the portico I shook my head slightly. There's a never-ending stream of Top Dog wannabes.

"I know this joint makes lots of cash," the wielder continued, waving the gun for effect. His other hand was in his pocket, like this was nothing to him. "You gon take me inside to the safe. You gon open it. You gon give me tha cash. Then I'm gon walk away. Do it my way and there aint no problems. Don' do it my way and I pull a double tap. Clear?"

The auto shop employee dropped the big plastic can and

172

the hollow *bonk* sound it made echoed off the two story strip mall wall. He nodded and instinctively raised his hands, then turned towards the open back door of the shop.

The *Imminence* spoke to me, and I followed the instructions. I sent an orb down the column and into the ground. It traveled the four miles in seconds and erupted under the feet of the gun wielder. He had lifted a foot to follow his victim, but it never came back down to the ground. Instead he shot straight up into the air, kind of like a bottle rocket. But he didn't whistle, he screamed.

The auto part guy turned in surprise, then watched in awe as his assailant flapped his arms wildly, like he thought it would help his current predicament. Upward momentum ceased at about thirty feet and, well, what you take away from gravity, you have to give back. The gun wielder then came back down to earth, but did not impact the ground. Instead he entered the giant trash bin at roughly twenty five miles an hour and made quite an explosion of unidentifiable food waste. Foam peanuts and pieces of plastic erupted from the bin like a small geyser.

For a full minute the auto part shop guy just stared at the bin, trying to determine what had just happened, but in the end, however, he decided he didn't care. That this was a much happier ending than what could have been. So he walked over to the bin and slowly looked with wide eyes over the rim.

His assailant lay there, covered in garbage, breathing but unconscious. The auto part guy suddenly had a dark thought and hoped the guy stayed unconscious until the garbage truck came in the morning, but then quickly stopped himself. That wasn't the kind of person he was.

Instead, he stared for a moment longer, then swirled his tongue around in his mouth. With much force he spit into the bin, then reached for the lid and slammed it closed. He then retrieved his trash can, entered the rear door of the auto parts store, then slammed that door closed as well.

I watched the empty backlot for a while longer, but sensed no other danger. Eventually I pulled my hands back and the orbs in my hands faded away. As they did so I suddenly had an overwhelming need for sleep. Turning, I headed back for the room, weariness pulling at my shoulders and eyelids.

I entered the room, then closed and locked the door. I returned to my bed, pulled my boots off, laid back on the thin, cheap pillows, pulled the threadbare bedspread over me as best I could, closed my eyes and said, "Return." The air became alive again, loosing its dead feel, and the water in the shower picked up where it left off.

I fought off sleep, waiting for Dara to finish her shower. The water finally turned off and I heard the shower curtain being snatched aside. I opened my mouth to say something out loud, but

Dara beat me to it.

"Rider?" she called out.

"Yeah?" I barked, sleep dragging my mind into a fuzzy, soft embrace.

"I closed the door all the way when I came in here, now it's open a few inches. Wanna explain that?"

Damn. "Later," I hollered as best I could. Only during Ranger school had I felt so tired. "Need sleep. Explain in the morning. Wake me in six hours."

A long pause, then, "Okay. But we need to go get me some new clothes in the morning, these are funky. Didn't have time to get mine from the car."

"Noted," I said, but it came out as a whisper. Then, as they call it in the army, the Z-Monster took me away.

*   *   *

I remember fading away and then it seemed only a few seconds before I awoke with Dara poking me in the shoulder. "Rider, its been six hours. Rider?"

I grunted myself awake. Opened my blues. Looked up at her. "I need clothes," she said, tugging at her shirt. Her hair was out of the ponytail, now only restrained by one of those thick, colorful rubber band things at the crown of her head. I don't know

175

what they're called, I'm not a fashion expert.

I pushed the cover off of me, blinked a few times, then sat up. I felt like a backhoe had driven over me. Swinging my size fourteens to the floor, I asked, "Did you sleep?"

Sitting on her own, rumpled bed, she nodded. "Like the dead. Glad they have wakeup calls, otherwise we'd both still be sleeping. So, want to tell me why the bathroom door was open when I got out of the shower?"

I looked at her and tried to blink sleep out of my eyes. Nodding, I leaned over to pull my boots on and, as I did so, told her what had happened at midnight. She seemed skeptical when I'd finished, so I raised my hands and summoned the orbs. They arose and sent flashes of light around the murky dimness of the room.

"This just gets weirder and weirder," she said, looking at the little balls of light.

"You're telling me," I said, and the orbs vanished. I rose, answered the call of nature, then went to my saddle bags and retrieved my toothbrush and toothpaste.

"That was sweet of you though. Worrying about me and all," she commented, then began pulling her own boots on over bare feet.

"Yeah, well, my middle name is Softy," I said. I oozed some paste onto my brush, then proceeded to brush the sweaters off my teeth. With diligence I brushed up and down, then side to side, making sure to brush my gums as well as tongue. Proper dental hygiene is of utmost importance in life. Then I rinsed, making sure to get any toothpaste foam out of my mustache, then returned the brush and tube to my bags.

"I need clothes," Dara repeated. "These smell disgusting, and I need new socks."

I stood at the edge of the bed I'd slept in for all of what seemed like a few seconds, then I nodded. "Okay, but first, breakfast. I'm starving."

"Are you ever *not* hungry?" my charge quipped.

We collected our belongings, which for Dara was only her helmet and items from her pockets, and we left the room. But as I pulled the door open, two men had handguns drawn, one pointed at me, the other at Dara.

Such was the start of our day. I sighed audibly.

My first thought was to wonder why the *Imminence* hadn't warned me, but then understanding came over me. These guys looked terrified. Their hands were shaking violently. One of them had tears in his eyes. They were both young, maybe early twenties, and both had the look of street rats. I guessed them to be drug runners. Probably they had arrest records, but not violent ones.

Their idling getaway car, a rusty, banged up Datsun, sat

behind them, doors open, muffler rattling, ready for a quick exit.

I dropped my saddlebags gently to the ground, then stepped in front of Dara and out onto the sidewalk. I stopped in front of them, their muzzles a foot from me. I then raised my hands, palms up, and made a slight nod with my head. "I know you're not going to pull those triggers boys, this is not who you are, I can sense it," I said quietly. "Just put them in my hands, get in your car, then drive away."

"But – we –," one of them said, the one with tears.

"Bock?" I asked.

They seemed surprised and glanced at one another, then the other one said, "He'll find us."

I shook my head. "He won't, I'll see to that. Just put them in my hands." After a long moment, they did, both with looks of relief on their faces. Being a petty criminal is one thing, being a murderer is another, and these two boys obviously didn't want to cross that line.

I looked at the weapons. Two Colts, old, banged up, probably dropped a hundred times, possibly retired military pieces when the army went with the Beretta.

I flipped them over, did a quick visual inspection, put their safeties on and then stuck them in my front jacket pockets. I then held my hands out to them. "Take my hands boys," I said as Dara stepped up beside me. The two kids looked at me like I was crazy.

"Look," I started to explain, "I haven't actually seen any of the bodies that seem to lie in the wake of Darian Bock, but from my understanding, it's not a pretty sight. Now you can take my hands, or you can be found tomorrow morning as two bags of meat in a Dumpster somewhere."

Men are, by nature, very visually oriented, something about hunting during our evolution, or something like that. I don't know, I'm not a biology kind of guy. But my words drew up a pretty nice visual for them, and it had the desired effect. They took my hands.

Changing Dara's colors took about thirty seconds, but with the new and improved *Imminence* pulsing in my brain, it only took about five. Just a few, small pulses of light, and it was done.

Then, for precautionary reasons, I did it again.

Then I let the boys' hands go, their eyes were wide. I put my own hands on the butts of the Colts. "You boy's need to find a better way in life, cause the one you're on only leads to concrete and steel, and big guys named Bubba who like young, skinny boys like you." Another visual for them to think about. " I suggest a community college. Try auto mechanic or HVAC, those jobs pay pretty well. Now git."

They wasted no time clambering into their ride and making a swift exit. If they could have laid rubber, I'm sure they would have, but the old Datsun engine just didn't have that kind of power anymore.

I watched them go, then turned towards Dara. "Fun way to start the day," she said, watching the car bounce violently out of the parking lot. She was standing about two feet from me, which made what happened next a bit awkward.

Over Dara's head, about fifty feet down the sidewalk, I watched a maid turn the corner and head in our direction. She was pushing one of those equipment carts that had a trashcan on one end and shelves full of tiny soaps and little bottles of shampoo on the other end. On top were piles of folded sheets and towels.

Black chrome swirled around her.

"Dang," I mumbled.

"What?" Dara asked, looking up at me. She had no choice, as I was almost a foot taller than her.

"Take one step towards me, and don't ask why." She hesitated for a moment, then complied and I felt our boots toes clunk together.

I made eye contact with the maid. She was a large woman, but looked well-toned. Our eyes locked long enough for both of us to know.

"Put your arms around me, put your head against my chest, and don't ask why." She complied, if somewhat reluctantly again. It meant her face was going to be buried in my beard. At least it smelled like shampoo.

Then in less than two seconds information was made known to me, from the new instruction manual in my skull. Initially I was going to pull the two Colts, flick their safeties off and put two rounds center mass of Molly the Maid. But the problem with this was I was unfamiliar with the Colts. Didn't even know if they were loaded, though I'm sure they were. Also, on some handguns the safety clicks on easier than it clicks off, a kind of safety of the safety, and I didn't know if that was the case with the Colts. Know your weapon like you know your cock, a Ranger Sergeant once barked in my face, though I would have said know it like the back your hand. That was during Ranger school, when I was six foot four and a buck eighty at best, a toothpick really.

But it turned out I didn't even need the Colts. Instructions came, and I followed. Two balls of light appeared in my hands and with one quick motion I sent them hurtling down the sidewalk – just as the maid pulled what looked like a double-barrel shotgun from under a folded sheet. It had a handle stock, not a shoulder one. It was a beast. She was quick, was able to get off a thundering shot, but the Seer Orbs deflected the buckshot in a flash of light. Thousands of little lead balls pinged, popped and ricocheted off the building, ground and, unfortunately, someone's parked car. The windshield shattered into a spiderweb pattern.

Then the orbs impacted the cart and maid.

The result did not go well for either.

Without any actual fire, the cart exploded violently, sending shredded pieces of plastic and cloth in every direction, and little soaps rained down. Simultaneously the maid caught the second orb in her chest. She was still holding the shotgun, but with wide eyes and an open mouth. She didn't explode with the impact, of which I was happy about. That would have been – messy. But she did go airborne for a good twenty feet, and her chest suddenly became unnaturally concave. Once she finished with her flying lesson, gravity won over and she rolled for a while before coming to a stop.

There was no movement.

Dara had turned to watch and I put a hand on her shoulder. There was a small pulse of light. Then another. "Did you just –," she started to ask, looking at my hand.

"Yes," I interrupted. "Bock discovered your new color, had to change it again. That's three in less than five minutes. We can assume there are more nearby, we need to go." I gathered my bags and moved swiftly to Lady T behind the fence, Dara asking questions along the way.

"Is she dead?" she asked, looking back at the still form on the sidewalk.

"I think that would be a reasonable assumption."

"What did that light thing do to her?"

"I would assume it turned her internal organs into something resembling ground beef, but I wouldn't know, I'm not a surgeon," I explained while pulling keys from my pocket.

"Can you do that any time?"

"You ask a lot of questions."

Arriving at the bike, I attached the saddlebags. Dara was pulling her helmet on as I pulled Lady upright. I heeled up the stand and Dara straddled the seat behind me. I started to put the key in the ignition slot, but then stopped. Some information unrolled in my mind and I thought about it for a moment. Then I put the keys back into my jacket pocket.

"What?" Dara asked.

I cocked my head over my shoulder. "Hold on, this is gonna get weird."

"Like this all hasn't been weird already?"

Without asking, the two orbs of light appeared in my hands. I looked at them for a long moment before turning my hands over and, slowly, grabbed the handlebars. "Don't go crazy, I like her the way she is," I muttered.

A yellow light emanated from my hands and into the handlebars. It made its way down the chrome bars and into the front forks, gas tank, engine and eventually both tires. Lady T glowed in the early morning light. I could feel Dara shifting behind me, trying to look down and see what was going on.

Looking down myself, I watched as little flecks of rust flaked off to reveal new chrome or paint. I saw the front tire and rim suddenly increase in diameter a few inches and felt the rear tire do the same thing, raising the whole bike by an equal amount. Popping and pinging caused me to look down at the engine and I watched as the whole block seemed to take a breath and expand, going from 750 to perhaps 900cc's. New tubes sprouted from the engine like tendrils, connecting with each other or other parts of the motor. Their purpose eluded me.

I felt, rather than saw, new rubber grips form under my hands and the seat under my rear inflate with new stuffing. It was time for a new one anyway as my arse had pulverized the stuffing yet again.

Then the light faded and the Lady started herself, no key needed. The guttural rumble that came from her engine was deeper now, a quiet thunder. Like a low warning growl from deep inside the throat of a lion.

"You got new saddlebags," Dara said with a muffled voice. I twisted and looked back. Nice, thick black leather. Chrome accents and buckles. The name "Triumph" was embroidered between the buckles in red. Looking over the bike again, I nodded. I thought dad would have been pleased.

I gave the Lady some gas, eased out the clutch and headed towards the front of the hotel. The exploded room cleaning cart was still there, and more or less everywhere. A shotgun lay amongst the plastic shrapnel, its barrel misshapen. A man in a tie was stooped down by the maid, appearing to feel for a pulse. He had a cell phone jammed to his ear, probably calling 911. His lips moved rapidly. He did not look up as we passed.

As we approached the parking lot exit, I pulled to the curb next to a water grate. Dara seemed to know exactly why as she reached around my waist, extracted the two Colts from my front pockets, leaned to one side and casually tossed them down the drain.

I pulled out onto SR70 and headed west, back towards I75. I popped cleanly through the gears, Lady taking the road eagerly with new, fat tires, her stallion engine purring like a quickened heartbeat. She seemed to beg that I open her up, twist the throttle all the way, but I kept her reigned in. All horses love to run, but there's a time and a place.

As the asphalt rolled away behind us, I listed the mission points for the day in my head: Food. Clothes for Dara. Take Dara to her uncle. Go find Bock.

A simple list really.

The first three would prove simple enough. Not so much the last one.

Four hours of life left. Unbeknownst to me.

185

16

7:25 a.m.

Sarasota, Florida

We stopped at Mary's Korner Kitchen for breakfast. The place was packed with overnight truckers; their eyes red, hair disheveled, clothes wrinkled, their rigs idling in the parking lot, chrome twinkling in the morning sun. The coffee was good and strong and hot. The eggs were served a little runny. The toast was extra crispy. The grits were super thick and creamy. But because they didn't offer shrimp with grits and cheese, I had to drop their overall rating in my head. Fine food otherwise, especially the runny eggs.

I dislike overcooked eggs.

I gently admonished the assistant manager about the shrimp thing. Hopefully she would take my heartfelt concerns to the manager or owner of the establishment and add grits with shrimp and cheese to the menu.

"You should start reviewing restaurants on Tripadvisor, you seem to have a thing for food," Dara explained as we left the restaurant.

"Tripawhoser?" I asked.

It's – you can – oh never mind," she said while yanking her yellow helmet on.

I pulled my own helmet on and brought Lady upright, popping back the kickstand. She started herself again as soon as I pulled the clutch handle back.

We pulled out of the parking lot, back onto SR70, and just a mile from I75, Dara patted me on the arm. I looked down to see and arm and finger adamantly pointing towards a strip mall to our right. I flicked the turn signal to indicate a right turn to the shiny BMW behind us.

It was a sad looking strip mall. Probably built when I was a kid, it had seen better days. Half the stores were shuttered with big banners in the windows advertising the square footage and phone numbers to call should you be interested. Another tap on my arm guided me to a store called JC's Closet, advertising that they were indorsed by some female Hollywood somebody or other. I didn't recognize the name.

I parked and Dara dismounted with enthusiasm and yanked her helmet off. "I love JC's!" she exclaimed. She almost danced, right there in the parking slip. "They have jamming clothes!"

I had no idea what jamming clothes were, but I said nothing, bowing to her expertise. I removed my helmet, then retrieved my hat from the new saddlebags. I swatted it open on my leg and tugged it on. We hung our helmets on the rear view mirrors and walked to the store entrance. Dara lead, I followed.

There was a display window facing the sidewalk, it had several mannequins in it, all facing away from the street, all with sweat pants or shorts on with slogans on their rear ends. One said HOT, another said FUNKY and yet another said YUMMY. I had no idea how to interpret the purpose of wearing pants of this nature.

My discomfort heightened as we entered the perfume-laden store. The air smelled of cold, air conditioned flowers and music played that I was pretty sure would make me insane had I had to listen to it for more than an hour. Extreme bass. High, screeching vocals. Lots of synthesizer background. It sounded like a hurricane was in the music business.

The four teen employees greeted Dara with smiles and a language I could not decipher, but they stopped short when they saw me follow behind her. Eight eyes glared at me like I was from another planet and Dara seemed to notice. "My big brother," she hollered over the music. "Don't worry, he's harmless, just don't make him angry."

I glared at each girl, one at a time and, in turn, they looked away, one at a time.

Dara hopped over to a rack of pink and white things, most

probably shirts, or blouses, or something. It was hard to tell because some of the shirts had hoods attached, which made no sense to me. Hood on a jacket, that I understand, but on a shirt?

Other shirts had frilly stuff on the sleeves and still others had big kiss prints on them that reminded me of the Rolling Stones logo. It was all very confusing.

I looked around, trying to find a place to sit while Dara did her thing, but the only things available were four giant plush chairs by the register, all vibrant pink. Making my way over to one, the two girls behind the counter picked up a conversation that had apparently been underway when we came in.

"So I said oh em gee, Gail, just friend him on eff bee or hit him up on Twitter," said one girl.

"Like, did she do it?" asked the other.

I lowered myself into the chair and the pink plastic squeaked and chirped. The padding was extremely thick and I could hear the air escape somewhere in a hiss as my bulk settled. It was like sitting on a giant balloon that was slowly deflating.

Then the first girl said, "I don't know, she hasn't texted me back yet, but oh em eff gee, she needs to get with the hip, you know?"

"Totally, I mean, double you tee eff?"

It was all very confusing and made my ears hurt, along with the music, so I tuned it out. I watched the other two girls for a while, they seemed to be the industrious ones. They darted with purpose from one rack or display to another, straightening disheveled shirts and refolding pants that had been picked up, unfolded, then rejected by a customer. At one point a telephone rang and one of the girls pulled a headphone set from around her neck and placed it over her ears. She touched a little button and greeted, presumably, a customer with a happy, cheerful voice.

The chair under me finally finished settling, my rear about a foot off the floor and my elbows, propped on the armrest, pointing up at forty-five degrees. I felt completely ridiculous, and the new song from the speakers wasn't helping. Some woman slamming out words incredibly fast about her boyfriend cheating on her, and that she was mad, and that he dissed her and she would find revenge.

I tuned it out again.

My focus moved from the two other employees and I watched as Dara picked out a few things. A shirt, short sleeve, some sort of red color. A pair of jeans. A package of socks. Some undergarments. All in all pretty conservative considering the store ambiance. Eventually she made her way over to me and held up the jeans and shirt. "Cool, huh?" she asked.

"The jeans are defective," I replied.

"What?" she asked, twisting the hanger back and forth while looking.

"Can't you see the holes?"

She smiled. "Those are supposed to be there, goof. It's the fashion."

This mystified me, as did the price tag dangling from a belt loop. Mine cost a third that price, and they were three times the size. "It's fashionable to buy jeans with holes already in them? That just makes no kind of sense. Why don't you just buy cheap jeans and I'll run over them with my bike a few times. Free of charge."

Dara's response was to stick her tongue out at me, turn in place and head off for the dressing room. She dressed swiftly, emerging after only a few minutes, her old clothes rolled in a ball.

She proceeded to the register while I tried to haul myself out of the chair. The armrests were so thick with padding it was hard to gain purchase to push upwards, but once I managed the seat hissed again as it refilled with air.

Dara handed the cashier a handful of little tags, then rummaged for her debit card. "You look – nice," I said, trying to be complimentary.

My young charge froze, then looked at me. "Wow, you actually said something kind and considerate."

The register made beeping sounds as I replied. "I'm always kind and considerate, just ask Dick from the restaurant last night."

Dara's brow wrinkled as she swiped her card through a little machine on the counter. "You knocked him out with a pan," she said. The cashier suddenly had a worried look on her face.

"Well, before that. I was very kind and polite to him. Things just went in a different direction than I had hoped. And it took more than one pan, I also had to use a soup pot."

The cashier handed Dara her receipt and in turn handed the cashier her ball of used clothing. "Will you throw these away?" Customer service usually requires one to do things they don't want to do, but you do it anyway. The girl behind the counter seemed to understand this policy and accepted ball like it was plutonium, then quickly dropped it into a small trashcan.

Once outside, we stopped and admired the new and improved Lady for a moment before I stowed my hat and we pulled on our helmets. Then we mounted up and headed out of the parking lot.

Within a few minutes Lady was pulling us comfortably north at sixty-five an hour, the wind blasting the residual perfume smell from from my nose. My right side warmed in the rising sun and the blue sky above was endless, marred only by a single, milky contrail from a jet airplane. As it was almost eight in the morning, rush hour traffic was starting to build, but that was fine by me, I just settled into the right lane and matched the speed of the car ahead. Just let the wind part around me.

"Only a cyclist knows why a dog sticks his head out the window, son," my dad used to say. I think he had a t-shirt with the slogan on it too.

I kept an eye on the rear-views, but nobody seemed to be following us and no black chrome made itself known to me. The *Imminence* itself was quiet as a whole, having tucked itself away after the Molly Maid incident.

Despite having only six hours of sleep, I felt good, refreshed. My belly and gas tank were full, two wheels were humming, the engine was purring and my four part check list was halfway done.

Tampa rolled closer.

17

Interstate 75 welcomed us northward. We passed exits for Palmetto and Bradenton, then the exit for I275 and the Sunshine Skyway. We passed exits that lead to Ruskin, Apollo Beach, Riverview and Brandon. We passed the exit for Interstate 4.

Soon after I received a pat on my shoulder. I looked to my side to see Dara's finger pointing at a sign: Bruce B. Downs Blvd. – 3 miles. I nodded and when the exit ramp appeared, I dropped through the gears and exited the highway.

Through a series of further shoulder taps and points, Dara guided me left, right, left, left, right again, until the last tap, a finger pointed at a house.

The house was a small one, a single level on a slab, perhaps two bedrooms, two baths, a small living room and an even smaller kitchen. It was a house based on a police officer's salary.

There was a single car garage and a front porch that might fit a couple chairs comfortably. It was obviously built back in the sixties, back when a big yard was more important than a big house. Kids played outside a lot more back in those days. And families did a lot more entertaining. Nowadays the bulk of new houses pushed the property lines.

There was a Dodge Charger in the driveway, its lightbar glinting in the morning sun, the Tampa Police logo stamped on the side.

I pulled in behind the car and shut the horses down. The silence after almost an hour of roaring wind, engine, tires and traffic was palpable.

As I was taking my helmet off, I felt the bike jerk sideways as Dara dismounted in a rapid fashion. I looked up to see a child, perhaps five years old, dashing out of the house and Dara running after her. They met on the porch and Dara dropped her helmet on the worn, dry wood. "Dawa, Dawa, Dawa!" the little girl hollered with glee and Dara dropped to sweep the child into an embrace.

I heeled down the stand and, carrying my helmet with me, dismounted and walked up the drive. As I arrived at the worn wooden step, a man came out of the house. He was tall and angular, fit and well groomed. The badge on his chest shone like a mirror, as did the sergeant stripes on his shoulder.

We made eye contact for a second longer than a moment, then he hugged Dara, who had stood, holding the little giggling girl in one arm.

"Hey Uncle Elroy," she said.

"Hey, kiddo," he replied. His voice was deep and strong.

Their embrace broke and Dara looked back at me and hooked a thumb. "This is Rider. His looks are deceiving. He's a softy really. Even paid me a compliment about an hour ago."

I stepped forward and we shook hands. "Pleasure," I said.

"Markus Elroy. Likewise," he replied, then studied me for a moment. "I'm going to guess ex military?"

I nodded. "Army. Rangers. Staff Sergeant. But that was a long time ago."

He smiled as we released hands. "Never really leaves you though, does it?"

I returned his smile. "No, I suppose not."

Dara made a few cooing sounds before turning to me again. "This is Carrie, my cousin."

The child looked at me. Her face was pink and her eyes were puffy, as if she'd only recently woken up. "Hi," I said, because I didn't know what else to say. My experience with children is exactly zero. Less than zero, actually. If it's possible to have *negative* experience with something, that would describe it even better.

"Daddy!" she said, pointing a finger at Elroy. Then, just as quickly, she said, "Dawa!" and pointed a finger at her much older cousin. This resulted in a poke in Dara's eye. Elroy and Dara chuckled, as did I, sort of. I'm not much of a chuckler.

"So," Elroy began, "this is a surprise visit. What's up?"

The smile on Dara's face faded. "We need to talk."

Elroy, being a cop, sensed something in her voice. "About?"

"Dad," she replied. There was a long pause and then she put Carrie down.

"Go back inside, sweetie," Elroy told the child, then patted her on the head. "Go play with your stuffed animals, we'll be right in."

"Yay!" she exclaimed and bolted for the door, pigtails flying.

I hooked belt loops and let Dara explain. "You know he was murdered for information he was gathering."

"Yes, has there been a break in the case?"

"No, they've yet to catch who did it, and probably never will. They're probably dead themselves now anyway."

"But?"

"But we know, Rider and I, we know who ordered the killing."

"Who?"

"A man named Darien Bock."

Elroy though for a moment, absently rubbing his chin, his

eyes intense. "Okay, that's the who, how about the why?"

Dara reached up and pulled the lanyard. When the flash drive popped out, she unclipped it and handed it to her uncle. "That answer will be on here."

"What's on it?" the sergeant asked.

"Don't know, it's password protected. He told me that if anything happened I should bring it to you."

Elroy's eyes fixed on the little finger-sized piece of plastic, then carefully took it from her, wrapping it in big fingers. He looked from Dara, to me, then back to Dara. "I just got off duty, let me change and we'll talk in the kitchen."

*   *   *

I sat at the kitchen table while Dara made coffee. The kitchen was indeed small, but it was clean and comfortable, almost homey.

A child's drawings were on the refrigerator, presumably Carrie's, and they were held in place with magnets shaped like flowers. A similar magnet held what looked like a small recipe card on the front edge of the vent hood over the stove.

There was a big bay window that looked out into the back yard. A requisite swingset was there, as well as a picnic table, a grill and a sagging aluminum shed, probably containing a lawnmower, folding chairs and miscellaneous yard tools, including a weed whacker. The yard was lush and green and well maintained with no vines growing up the encircling chain link fence.

The little machine on the counter burbled and sputtered and soon coffee aromas filled the room.

After fifteen minutes, Elroy came into the kitchen. He'd put on a newer pair of blue jeans and a t-shirt that proclaimed his loyalty to the Tampa Bay Buccaneers. "I called Claire down the street," he said. "She's going to babysit Carrie for the afternoon."

"Cwaire!" Carrie shouted from the living room.

Elroy had also brought a laptop with him and he placed it carefully on the table. Dara brought coffee cups to the table along with a little dish with sugar in it. Then she retrieved a little spouted cup of milk and the coffee pot itself, which she placed on one of those heat-resistant pads.

I couldn't remember the last time I sat at an actual kitchen table for coffee, perhaps with Cora a few years ago. I was also a little out of sorts with how to prep my coffee without pre-portioned sugar packets and creamers, but I managed.

We each fixed coffee's to our own liking and made small talk. Elroy said he liked my bike, and I said thank you. I said his back yard looked nice and clean cut, and he said thank you. Dara had opened the laptop, punched some buttons, then told us it was probably going to rain sometime this morning. Elroy and I grunted.

"How long were you in?' Elroy asked.

"Almost four years. You?" He didn't ask what almost meant.

"Just three, got out just before Desert Storm, went to the academy." Juggling the dates in my head, I determined he was in his mid forties.

"What branch?"

"Army. Enlisted. Just a grunt. Never made it past Specialist." A grunt typically meant an Infantryman, because they grunt a lot carrying sixty pound rucksacks on their backs for days on end.

"Aunt Wendy already at work?" Dara asked. I assumed that was Elroy's wife.

The Sergeant nodded, "She's got first shift this week. Left just a few minutes before you got here."

Eventually the doorbell rang and Carrie was up in a shot. "Cwaire!" she hollered again, running to the door with a stuffed animal in each hand. Elroy and Dara both went to the door, Elroy to open it, Dara to give Carrie a goodby hug. When they returned it was just the three of us, three steaming mugs and a quiet house.

There was a long moment of silence between us, two of us preparing to talk, one preparing to listen and ask questions. "So, tell me about this Bock," Elroy said eventually.

And so Dara told him, starting six weeks ago with her father's death. Two weeks after that Bock started sending his goons after her. At least twice a week she'd barely escaped another attempt at catching her. Or worse.

Her uncle listened carefully, asking to clarify or additional information. To a police officer, details are like bread crumbs, the more the better.

She also told him about us meeting in the North Port home, and the goons that came in afterward. Then came the story of our getaway from the karate wannabes, the guys in the Lincoln, then the attempted hit at the hotel earlier that morning.

Sergeant Elroy pinched his chin with thumb and forefinger, riding every word carefully. "That level of ineptitude sounds highly unlikely, from before you two met. Sounds like he was trying to keep you on the run, not catch you."

"That's what Rider said," replied Dara.

The big man looked at me.

"He was using Dara to get to me, he used her to flush me out," I explained. "Yes, he want's that flash drive, but he want's me too. So he kept her on the run, knowing eventually our paths would cross."

"Those are some pretty low odds, there's a lot of people in Florida. Odds become even lower in that she was in hiding all the time."

I shook my head. "Bock wasn't using her to eventually find me. His goal was for me to find her instead. And it worked. And things changed once we were together. The gloves came off, as did the safeties of a lot of guns. Bock placed those guys as soon as you arrived at the North Port home," I said, looking to Dara. "How long were you there before I came?"

She shrugged. "Couple hours, I guess."

I nodded. "You can bet those guys were in place within half an hour of you holing up. They were probably in another house, right across the street, or next door. If I'd have decided not to stay at that house and moved on, those guys would have flushed you on the run again."

"Why does he want you so bad?" This was from the Sergeant.

"I'm a threat to him."

"How?"

"I'm – I can –," I started, but I broke off. I figured I could try to explain, but in the end I thought it better just to show him. So I calmly placed my hands on the dark oak table, palms up. Then I summoned the orbs and they gently appeared, hovering over my palms, their lights flashing softly on the walls and ceiling.

Sergeant Elroy stared blankly. No shock, no surprise, no

worry. Just a steadfast stare of a seasoned police officer who had seen everything at least once, perhaps more than twice, and surely a lot worse.

"Interesting," was his only reply. "What are they?"

I took a deep breath, thankful of his clear mind. "I have a gift, or it was given to me, I'm not sure. I have the ability to see imminent danger, or people in distress, and I step in to help," I explained. "These orbs are a tool, a means to that end." I let the orbs fade away.

The Sergeant was not an ignorant man. I watched his keen eyes dart back and forth for a moment, connecting the dots. "So, you're *that* Rider. Wanted by pretty much every police precinct in the state of Florida, including the Florida Highway Patrol."

I nodded.

He paused, looking me right in the eyes. "You've killed a lot of people."

I nodded, then added, "Every one of them in self defense, or to save the life of an innocent."

The Sergeants eyes were hard. "A few moths ago I investigated an attempted robbery and shooting. Jacky Jay's. Was that you?"

I nodded. "The one I shot was probably going to cut that girl. I knocked the other guy out."

The Sergeant nodded. "You broke his jaw. He's in jail. He

had warrants. The girl's description of you was way off, as well as dozens of others that I know of. Why?"

Dara sat quietly, just listening and absently sipping coffee, turning her head back and forth, depending on who was speaking.

"That's where it gets complicated. I have a – team – that assists me. Only recently met them. They – alter the memories of the victims, and eyewitnesses, in order to protect my identity. So I can continue to help people."

The Sergeant looked at me for a long time, long enough to pick up his coffee twice to sip. He was leaning back in his chair, one hand in his lap, the other holding his mug. After a moment, he looked at Dara, then back at me. "You realize I could lose my career, maybe even go to jail myself for not arresting you, right now. Aiding and abetting a criminal, or harboring a fugitive."

Shaking my head, I said, "I'm not asking for aid, and you aren't harboring me. I'm just a guy who rides a motorcycle. Who brought you your niece. Who was in imminent danger."

Again the Sergeant was quiet for a spell, then, "I do not condone what you do, Mr. Rider, or whatever your real name is.

"And I didn't ask for this gift, or curse as I sometimes feel that it is. It is, as was so recently pointed out to me, my destiny. I am not a liberty to walk away from this path. I am compelled; commanded. It is who I am."

Elroy took another sip of coffee, as did I, as did Dara. The

Sergeant then reached into his jeans pocket and pulled out the flash drive. Dara rotated the laptop and pushed it towards him, then both she and I moved our chairs to better see the screen.

Elroy clicked the little drive open, exposing a silver tongue, then slipped it into a small port in the side of the laptop. A little popup appeared after a moment, asking if he wanted to open the drive. Elroy clicked yes. Another popup appeared, asking for a password.

"Shit," he said, and stared at the screen a long time.

"Has to be something you would know easily," Dara suggested.

"And I think I know what it is," he replied and thought for a while longer. Then he leaned forward and typed, little black dots appeared in a square on the screen. It was a lot of dots and when he finished he clicked OK and a file page opened.

"What was it?" Dara asked.

"Your father and I played Jr. Varsity football together in high school. He was a sophomore and a wide receiver. I was a junior and a quarterback. Last play of the game against Berkshire High. We were down by five. It was your dad's idea to run a play called Eighty Five Panther. Eighty five being your dad's number and panther because he could run like one. Said he could beat the cornerback and free safety. He did, shot down the seam at full sprint, beat his coverage. I threw it, he caught it, we won. The password was 'eightyfivepanther.'"

The file page contained several folders. I knew this because they looked like little yellow folders. At least that's what I assumed as I'm not very good with computers. My only real experience came from stopping at libraries to look up local motorcycle shops in the rare event that Lady went down and I wasn't near Miami. Even then a librarian had to help me.

The folder names were confusing, just a jumble of letters, numbers and underscores. Perhaps they were file numbers from actual paper copies. Case numbers, or something like that.

But besides the file folders, there was a plain document who's name I could read very well. It said, simply, 'Markus.'

The sergeant rubbed his finger on a pad, moving a little pointer over the file, then double clicked a little button. The computer thought about this request, courteously giving us a little spinning timer to say wait a moment, then the file popped open.

Elroy leaned forward to read, then leaned back again. There was an obvious pained expression on his face. A note from the grave, from the beyond – from his brother. How does one prepare to read such a communication? The surviving brother took a breath and steeled his jaw, then leaned forward again. Dara and I made eye contact, then leaned back in our own chairs, giving Elroy a bit of privacy. This note, if it contained any personal words, was not for us.

Elroy read for a while, then scrolled down. Read some more, then scrolled again. This happened twice more before he scrolled back to the top and started over. His eyes remained expressionless, but I could see jaw muscles tighten below his ear.

After the second read through, he cocked sideways and wrested a smart phone from his front pant pocket. As he touched a series of buttons, he said, "Good timing, it's going down this morning, right here in Tampa." Then he held his phone to an ear, his eyes returning to the computer screen.

I heard a voice come through the phone, then Elroy said, "Carol, put me through the the Chief." A pause, then, "Sir, Sergeant Elroy here. I have just been given reliable information of an extreme nature. We have an emergency bio-hazard situation. We need to initiate immediate evacuation of Apollo Beach, specifically Suncoast Marina."

After a pause, the sergeant said, "Ricin, sir. Ricin gas."

18

8:45 a.m.

Tampa, Florida

Elroy said nothing after the phone conversation, just left the kitchen and headed to the back of the house, presumably to put his uniform back on. I myself stood and walked out into the living room as Dara put away the remains of our coffee and accompanying items.

I stopped at the big bay window that overlooked the front yard and hooked my thumbs. The once sunny morning had become overcast with dingy gray clouds. Darker thunderstorms seemed to be building in the west, coming in off the Gulf.

A car backed out of the driveway across the street, a newer Ford something-or-other, it's driver probably heading off for the nine to five grind.

Half a block up the street a lumbering school bus stopped at a corner and engulfed three children. Its maw then closed, its air brakes hissed, black smoke billowed from the exhaust and it crossed before my eyes as it proceeded to the next stop.

But I hardly registered any of it, instead my eyes were

locked on the road itself.

I always thought that destiny was supposed to be a pretty thing, a road paved in gold that led us on to something greater in our lives. For many years I assumed that if it were anything else, then you were on the wrong road. I'd never worried about it too much though, I was happy with the road I was on, be it made of black asphalt, or concrete.

But recent events now clearly told me that destiny is not always pretty, that it can be a dark, bumpy road. And sometimes a lonely one. Events also told me that I had been following my destiny all along, even though I was not consciously aware of it, and even though the road was not made of gold.

And now the next miles in the path of my destiny lay before me, outside the window, beyond the porch, and beyond the yard. The road that was just a road when we arrived, was now a ribbon of black chrome.

And I instinctively knew where it would take me.

Clinking in the kitchen behind me had stopped, and I became aware of Dara's eyes on my back, but I did not turn. "You're leaving, aren't you?" she asked.

I nodded to the window, my reflection barely visible. "You know my policy. Next town down the road, then the place after that."

"You're going after Bock?"

I shrugged. "If that's where the road leads me." My voice sounded unusually loud as it reverberated off the glass pane before me.

Booted feet came down the hallway and I turned to see Sergeant Elroy enter wearing a standard police field uniform. He was just holstering his weapon as he came to a stop next to Dara, then looked up at me. "Thank you for bringing Dara to me, Mr. Rider."

I turned half a step. "You're welcome."

He put his hands to his hips, took a step towards me, then sighed. "I do not condone what you do, it goes against what I believe. That laws are on the books for a reason. I should arrest you, but I'm not going to. Firstly I don't have time, and secondly I have a feeling that trying to arrest you would be like trying to put a leash on a grizzly bear." He said the last part with a slight smile.

I didn't reply.

"Just – you know – try not to kill so many people. Subdue and secure. Let the law take care of the rest."

"I'll – see what I can do," I replied, then moved to the couch to retrieve my helmet. It lay on the cushion like an upside down turtle.

I picked it up, stood, and found the Sergeant still looking at me. He sighed again, looked at the floor, then explained, "In case you're wondering what you risked your life for. They're

210

smuggling ricin through a port in Tampa. Its destination is New York. Whoever 'they' are plan on releasing the ricin in Central Park, where it will kill thousands. Thousands more not killed will suffer lifetime ailments. Bock seems to be the organizer, but the mastermind appears to be a Senator in D.C. Name as yet unknown."

"To what end?" I asked.

He hesitated before answering, his eyes stern. "An excuse for the United States to use micro-nuclear munitions against Al-Qaeda and any other extremist Islamic group. Trillions of dollars have been spent for war in the ten plus years since 9/11. Seems this senator wants to stop that leak once and for all. With a decisive blow. Release ricin in Central Park, blame it on an Islamic group. Excuse to strike with extreme prejudice achieved."

"What's a micro-nuke?" Dara asked.

The sergeant shook his head and looked to his niece. "Don't know, not my line of work. Must be something very low yield, or something that disperses or degrades quickly. After inflicting its damage that is. Anyway, the whole circus has been notified and are converging on Apollo Beach as we speak. The ricin will never make it out of Tampa."

We all stood, saying nothing for a long moment. Dara fiddled with her hands, I inspected my helmet, the sergeant adjusted his gun belt.

I glanced back out at the road. It still shimmered like a black, mirrored river. "I have to go," I said, turning back to Elroy, "my bike is in your way anyway."

The sergeant nodded and extended his hand, I took it. "Stay safe out there," I said.

"You as well," he replied, without a smile.

Our hands dropped and Dara approached me. She looked up, I looked down. Then she hugged me, her head even with my sternum, her cheek buried in my beard. I think she sniffed back a tear before saying, "Thanks for beating back the boogeymen."

I'm not very good at intimate situations, but I put my arms around her small form and returned the hug in a way I thought appropriate. "You're welcome," I said for the second time.

"And for shopping with me."

I smiled. "Not something I care to repeat."

We broke our embrace. "Stop by anytime," Dara offered, her eyes moist. Her hands began fidgeting again.

"I'll keep that offer in mind," I replied as both Elroy and I made our way to the door.

"Oh, one more thing?" Dara asked. I stopped and turned. "What's your real name?"

I hesitated before responding. "Bix. Bix Reel," I replied.

Dara seemed to think on this for a moment, then nodded.

Elroy and I then left. We said nothing to each other as I

pulled my plastic skull on and lashed it under my chin, trying not to get beard hair caught in the buckle.

I mounted my steed and the sergeant dropped inside his cruiser. New Dodge Charger, black and white and shiny, despite the sun being behind clouds. It sat low and menacing. Probably a three-forty, Hemi V-8 under the hood. A thundering beast in any pursuit, and a car reserved for the more seasoned veterans.

I pulled Lady upright and heeled back the stand. I started to reach for the keys in my pocket, but stopped. Instead I squeezed the clutch and the engine turned over, a throaty growl from the tailpipes. I let her roll backward into the street and turned so I was facing east, then tapped the transmission into first. I looked one more time up at the house, and saw Dara standing at the bay window where I had been earlier.

She waved with her left hand and used a knuckle on her right to push a tear away.

I held her gaze for a moment longer, then lowered my face shield, gave Lady the clutch and gas she begged for, and we headed down the street. Behind me Sergeant Elroy backed his car out, then headed in the opposite direction. Before me a chrome river led me to the next point in my destiny, *Imminence encounter* 359.

And the last two hours of my life.

And the inbound thunderstorms followed.

19

9:45 a.m.

Tampa, Florida

The past is gone, faded into a sepia colored series of photographs in our minds. The future is unknown, a blank pile of empty pages, waiting to be written upon. The present is imminent, the point in which we live our lives and make decisions about what will be written on those pages.

The current page being written had Lady firing her cylinders, pumping energy through the drive train, to the rear wheel. Then the rear wheel pulled gray, faded asphalt from the future, to the present, then left it in the past.

The *Imminence* guided us back south on I-75, then exited on I-4 eastbound. In my rear-view mirrors I could see the storms and flashes of lightening coming in off the ocean, chasing us inland. It looked as if Thor was in a fury, smashing his hammer on the anvil of the clouds.

Within twenty minutes a sign appeared on the shoulder of I-4. Lower Green Swamp Preserve Road, it said, Maintenance Vehicles Only, Not An Exit. But the black chrome instructed otherwise, so I slowed.

The ramp was blocked with tall, concrete partitions, but there was room on the far right side that I was able to squeeze Lady through. The exit ramp was littered with leaves and clumps of grass growing from fractures in the pavement, but nothing to threaten air-filled tires.

At the top of the ramp I turned left and headed north. I kept the bike at thirty as there were palm fronds, branches and small potholes on the ill-maintained road. And the two lane road was a lonely one with no guardrails or light posts. No buildings at all either; just choppy pavement with a faded double-yellow line running down the middle.

The air reeked of rotting vegetation mixed with a hint of sulfur.

At one time the shoulders of the road may have been mowed and maintained, but now scrub palm and small pine trees dominated right up to the emergency lanes, shedding their leaves and needles. Mother nature, reclaiming what was once hers.

I drove on for about five miles until I saw a sign. Lower Green Swamp Preserve, Closed To The Public, it said. Underneath this it stated, Maintained By The Florida Bureau Of Land Management. Before the recession, it may very well have been maintained, but Florida, as with other states, had to put things on hold, or close them temporarily, even seven years later.

The building behind the sign was dilapidated to the point of being unserviceable. It had probably been locked up for five years at this point, and it showed. Peeling paint, sagging porch, broken windows, crowded by scrub from all sides. The paint may have been Government Green at one time, but now had faded to a moldy color. The Florida sun is unforgiving.

I slowed and looked, but didn't stop, the *Imminence* guided me further down the road.

Lady stayed in lower third gear and she hummed along, her tires going *bop-bop* over the occasional palm frond branch, or through a small pothole. The only other sound was my breathing.

At one point I put Lady in neutral, planted my feet and shut the engine down, then flipped my face shield up. The silence was deafening. Not even a breeze rustled the trees, nor could I even hear the whisper of distant cars and rigs on I-4 far behind me. For a moment I thought time had come to a standstill again, until a fat drop of water landed on top of my helmet.

The storm was pending.

I started Lady up again and we moved forward. I left my face shield up. We cruised along for maybe another two calm, quiet miles before things got rather peculiar.

The land around me somewhat cleared and a small, abandon village appeared on my left. I read a heavily weathered sign that said, Thonotosassa Historical Site, and something about

Seminol Native Americans when suddenly I was no longer riding Lady down a long quiet road.

Instead, something slammed into me from my right and I found myself airborne. Limbs flailing, my view flashing between sky and ground, sky and ground. I caught a glimpse of Lady, also spinning and floundering, her wheels still turning.

We must have been thrown pretty high, as the falling part seemed to take a long time. "Damn," I said inside my helmet. Not exactly a curse word, but one I saved for very unique occasions, and this certainly seemed to fit he bill.

Fifty or so feet later the ground and I met in a most thundering and violent way. There was no bouncing or rolling, just a dead on slam into the hard, sandy, Florida soil.

Then I heard Lady impact somewhere nearby, and it was not a pretty sound. There was a din of metal being rent and twisted, plastic being shattered and glass breaking. Eventually the wreckage came to a stop and I was greeted with absolute silence. With the silence I became aware that I was still alive, still breathing. How that was possible, I had no idea, but I didn't argue the point.

My helmet was full of dirt and dust and I reached up and unlashed the strap, then pushed it off. My brain then went into damage control. I had moved my arms, no problem, so I moved my legs. No problem. I breathed in again. No problem. Heart beating? A bit hard and louder than usual, but still pumping away.

"Then get off your bum, soldier," I said to myself. And so I did. First I sat up, then rolled sideways and planted first a hand, then a boot. Dirt and grit fell from my hair and beard. Pushed myself up and planted a second boot. Shook the fog from my head and took another breath, then opened my eyes.

I was facing the way I had come, the road about fifty feet away. The road itself, as well as the ground between it and myself, was shattered, like a broken car windshield. Like an underground bomb had been detonated.

I could not see what had hit me.

As I looked, my hands absently brushed dirt and grime from my beard, shirt and jacket.

Then I turned my head and saw Lady, or what remained of her, and I caught my breath. Walking over I found her in dozens of pieces. A mirror here, a fender there, a tire in one place, a tailpipe in another. The front forks had broken off and came to a rest against a small tree. My saddlebags lay in the depression of the initial impact, their content scattered about.

The main body of the bike looked like it had been run over by an eighteen wheeler and the smashed gas tank leaked fuel onto the ground. For a moment my mind flashed back to my father and I rebuilding her, all those years ago. I doubted even my father's persistence could have rebuilt her this time.

The rear tire was still spinning, slowly, the spokes tick-ticking in the weeds.

The engine itself pinged as steel and aluminum cooled.

One of the tailpipes, still scalding hot, caused wisps of smoke as it scorched dry, dead leaves.

Lady T was no more.

I looked down, away from the carnage and found that my hat had come out of one of the bags and now lay on the ground at my feet. It was tan in color and stood out against the dark, organic dirt and dead grasses. I bent down to pick it up, slapped it into shape against my leg, then pulled it on.

As I adjusted it I saw something else that had come out of the bags. And old picture, cracked and creased and yellowed with age. I stepped over to it and picked it up. I looked at the picture of a child from almost thirty years ago, smiling and leaning and grabbing handlebars. It seemed like a hundred lifetimes ago.

I pulled my jacket open and tucked the picture into my left breast pocket, then turned my head away and remained quiet for a moment.

And then I got mad. And I gritted my teeth. And it made the muscles in my temples hurt.

I don't like getting mad, it's a wasted emotion that can lead to poor or irrational decisions. And right now, I needed a clear mind. So I closed my eyes and took a long breath, and then another, and yet a third, and I let the *Imminence* come to the front of my mind. The colors came to life in my eyes, conveyed information, suggested courses of action.

It also told me I was no longer alone.

Then I opened my eyes and turned to face him. "Hello Bock," I said. I was surprised at how small he was, just standing there, with arms crossed and a look of bemusement on his face. How he'd approached without me hearing I did not know. I suppose I was distracted.

His business-sense cut black hair was combed back neatly over a high, smooth forehead. The overall milky complexion of his face said he didn't spend a whole lot of time outdoors. He wore a white shirt under a faded denim jacket with likewise colored jeans. He looked like someone who probably got bullied in school, but now radiated confidence.

"Rider," was all he said.

I looked over my shoulder at my bike, then back at him. I summoned the orbs, but kept my arms by my side, and felt them arise from my palms. Bock didn't move, just stood and looked at me. "I had that bike for a long time," I said.

Bock shifted sideways a bit so he could see behind me. I saw his eyes dart from one part to another, making a show of actually studying them, then he looked back at me. He said, "You won't be needing it anymore, anyway," then just stared at me with his mouth slightly open, a curious look in his eyes. Like I was an enigma or something, like I was a bug that had just been doused with insect killer, yet still kept crawling around.

"Your plan, with the ricin. It failed. They'll have intercepted the boat by now."

Bock rolled his shoulders in a sloppy shrug. "Not my problem. I kept you occupied long enough to get my payment."

The sky darkened further and a few more fat rain drops exploded on the dusty ground. Bock took two steps to my left and I turned to stay facing him.

"Those are cute, by the way," he said, nodding to the orbs still alight in my hands. Then he snorted a laugh. "You look like a weird gunslinger or something." Then he reached one hand forward, palm up. Immediately a small yellow orb appeared, hovered there for a moment, then quickly ballooned to the size of a basketball.

Then it turned to black chrome.

"Mine's bigger than yours, Little Red Riderhood," he said, then flicked his hand. His orb crossed the ten foot distance between us quickly.

But the *Imminence* had told me to expect this, and my own hands were already moving. The orbs left my palms and impacted the black mass just three feet from me, and the concussive force sent me airborne again.

"Great," I muttered. As I flew up and backwards, getting ready to impact who knows what, I at least had the pleasure of seeing Bock knocked down.

What I impacted turned out to be an old barn. I know this because after crashing through a wall, skidding across the hayloft planks and plummeting to the floor, I opened my eyes to see piles of long-dried cow manure. They were ancient and dried and dusty, but thankfully no longer smelled.

I lay there for a moment, on my back, doing another damage control check. Results all okay.

Despite the clouds outside, beams of light penetrated through cracks and gaps in the barn's siding. The weak rays of light looked smokey with all the dust kicked up from my violent entry. The sheet-metal roof pinged and ponged with fat raindrops playing a unique percussion.

Then the double doors at the far end opened. They popped and cracked on old hinges and I turned my head in that direction. Bock stood there, backlit by the weak outdoor light, his hands holding the doors open. "You should be dead twice now," he said with a touch of curiosity in his voice.

"Yeah, well, I like to think of myself as a resilient guy," I said while pushing myself off the ground, broken boards falling to the floor. "And someone once suggested that my arse it made of granite."

Bock actually chuckled, then said, "I'm thinking maybe you have a little assistance. How's the team these days, that old bat Constance still taking care of the other three decrepit idiots?"

I planted a boot and made like I was going to answer the question, but as soon as both hands were off the ground I summoned and launched two orbs in less than half a second. Bock raised his hands in surprise, but my aim was a bit off. Instead of hitting him, the bright, yellow orbs hit either door. They exploded in spectacular fashion, sending Bock backward in a rain of splintered wood.

It was clear I was going to have to work on my aim.

As the dust settled, I reached down and picked up my hat, dusted it off and put it back on. Then a loud bang came from my right, like a gunshot.

Unfortunately for me, my actions proved too much for the old barn. More loud bangs echoed in the cavernous building as rotted foundation beams began to splinter, groan, and give way. I made to run for the ruined doors, but I'd only taken two steps when that entire wall came down in a thundering crash. Turning, I looked for another exit, but saw none.

"Dang," I said again and looked up. Two other walls quickly gave way and I watched the massive roof support beams give way to gravity. It looked like whole trees were used for the beams, possibly pine, but I'm not sure. I'm not a botanist.

But irregardless of the make and model of these particular trees, one thing was for sure, I was in their way of complying with gravity. But before they could flatten me to a Riderburger, I flicked two more orbs straight upwards. They contacted the beams and roof itself and blasted a massive hole through the plunging structure, then I found myself in a thundering whirlwind of shattered wood, twisted metal and choking dust.

I quietly hoped it wasn't powdered cow poo I was breathing, but it probably was.

Opening my eyes, I found my head just poking through the hole I'd made, the once proud roof now encircling me, sitting atop demolished walls.

Using two unbroken support beams as a ladder, I climbed up through the hole and balanced on the ridge. Dust was still settling as I took a moment to smooth my beard down, pieces of splintered wood fell away and pinged off the metal roof in cadence with the rain drops.

Remarkably, my hat was still on my head.

Then I looked to the west to see the anvil-like storms were almost upon us, blue lightening alighting them from within, angry thunder echoing from their depths. I also saw Bock in the same direction, about twenty yards away. His clothes were a bit roughed up and his hair could have used a good combing, but otherwise he seemed none the worse off. He was just standing there, with another black orb in his hand. He was gently tossing it up and down, the bemused look was back on his face.

I looked down at the shattered roof before me, took a couple steps to the left and jumped. The wooden heels of my boots offered no resistance as they crashed down on the metal and I extended my arms for balance as I surfed the corrugated metal and slid to the ground.

Then I summoned two orbs.

"This the game plan?" I hollered at Bock, my deep voice reverberating off other, nearby, dilapidated buildings. "We're just going to blast at each other all day? That'd be mighty rude, destroying such a nice historical site and deprive kids of a field trip."

The raindrops started falling faster now, their impact on the dusty soil looked like bullet ricochets in old western movies, reminding me of Saturday morning Lone Ranger marathons. Way before my time, of course, but my father insisted they were timeless.

We stared at each other over parched ground, half-dead scrub plants and pieces of lumber from the now-fallen barn. Distant thunder rolled over our heads like an airborne freight train.

Eventually I said, while walking towards him, "You could have been a force for good, Bock. Why'd you turn away?"

I stopped my approach ten yards from him.

Bock looked at the orb hovering over his hand, then made a twisting motion with his wrist. The orb began to spin. "I was like you once, Rider. I was happy going around rescuing people, punishing the bad guys. For twelve years I did it, but then I grew weary. What was *I* getting out of it? Where was a my reward for being such a positive force?" he asked, then shook his head slightly. "No, I got tired of being a puppet. Got tired of driving around in an old, rusted Pontiac playing the part of some sort of ridiculous avenger. And if I did it long enough, what? I'd retire and sit in some dumpy old house in Ireland?"

He smiled and spun his fingers again before continuing. "Not for me, Rider. After twelve years I wanted some payback, some sort of reward for dedicating my life to being the puppet of the Overseers and Governors," he explained, then looked up at me. "Did Constance give you that shit about destiny?"

I did not reply.

"I'm sure she did, but she's wrong. I changed my destiny, Rider. So can you. You don't have to be a puppet, you can choose your own destiny, your own future."

"I like my life, and my destiny," I explained. "I like helping people, and beating down the bad guys." The wind was picking up and both our jackets flapped in the turbulence.

Bock nodded. "For now, for now," he repeated in a

resigned voice. "But what are you getting in return Rider? What's your reward for being a puppet?"

"Good deeds don't necessitate reward, Bock. Besides, the look of gratitude in the eyes of people I help is reward enough."

Bock laughed out loud, the orb in his hand still spinning. A particularly loud crack of thunder vibrated the ground beneath our feet. The smell of ozone filled my nostrils. "Are you that gullible, Rider?" Bock asked. "Are you that deluded?"

I ignored both questions. "You could have walked away, surrendered your powers back to the Overseers."

But Bock was shaking his head. "I used my powers for twelve years helping others, now I'm using it to help myself. Turnabout is fair play, right?"

"Helping yourself do what?"

But Bock didn't answer. Instead he squatted down, turned his hand over and slammed the orb into the earth. The ground thundered with its impact.

Things got interesting after that.

The ground responded immediately and welled up before Bock, like a giant animal arising from the earth. It grew to about ten feet in height and I could see the rocks and dirt roiling in the animated mass.

Then it came at me, fast, like a massive wave rolling through the ground. And it got bigger as it got closer, quickly tripling my height and growing twenty or more feet wide.

Now I knew what threw Lady and I airborne.

No way I could outrun it, so I did the only thing I could think of, I loosed my own orbs at it as fast as I could.

The affect was minimal, blasting two holes through the brown, porous mass, that quickly closed again. I turned my head away as it impacted me and for the last time that day, I went airborne again.

"Should get a cape with all this flying around," I said as I face planted against the upper floor what appeared to be a home, though I wasn't sure, as I was moving rather quickly to notice. The old wood siding gave way easily as I entered the structure. There was a moment of empty space as I flew through a room, then I became intimate with an interior wall, this one harder with plaster and latticework. It didn't stop my forward progress, but slowed my bulk enough to hit the floor once I was through.

The floor I landed on was the second floor landing. I knew this because I skidded across the floor and crashed through a bannister railing, resulting in a one way ticket to the first floor. The impact did more harm to the old floor planking than me.

After the rest of the broken bannister followed me down, I rolled over onto my back, opened my eyes and looked around. It was indeed a home and was probably pretty nice at one time. There is a name for the main house on a plantation, but I don't know what it is. I'm not a historian. Whatever they're called, this must have been one.

I may not have known what the house was called, back in its day, but there was one thing I did know: Bock was beating me like an old area rug hanging on a clothes line.

I looked at the destroyed flooring around me, then up at the shattered bannister. I couldn't see the two holes I'd put in the walls upstairs, but I felt bad about the damage. The taxpayer was probably going to foot the bill for repairs. And I felt bad about that too.

Pushing the broken banister off me, I sat up, then pushed myself up on booted feet. My jacket was in tatters by now, so I shrugged it off, let it fall to the floor. Turning, I found a door leading outside. Old door, but with new deadbolt to resist squatters and mischievous teens. Thankfully the deadbolt had a twistlatch on the inside, otherwise I would have had the break the door down, and I didn't want to do that.

Once out onto a shabby front porch, I pulled the door closed behind me. No way to relock it.

I then stepped to the edge of a three step staircase and said to myself, "Time to get serious, soldier."

The first thing I did was close my eyes and let the *Imminence* unfurl in my mind. The flashes and lights had been in my vision all along, but with all the flying lessons I was taking, it

229

was hard to stop and understand what they were trying to convey.

Now they conveyed plenty as my now hatless head and beard hair rustled and lifted in the increasing wind. I could see a flash of light through my eyelids, then heard a long peal of rolling thunder, then felt the vibrations through my boot heels.

The rain then came down unabated. Thor's hammer finally cracked the anvil.

The old porch protected me from the direct rain, but swirling mist soon soaked my beard.

Without opening my eyes, I turned to a support beam that held the upper floor eight feet off the ground. I summoned two orbs and grabbed the old wood. It was soft under my calloused hands. The orbs sank deep.

The *Imminence*, like the night before, opened the world around me and I freed my mind to it.

There. Bock. On the other side of the house. In the pouring rain but not seeming to notice. Walking towards the sad, antique home.

I tried to time it just right. The orbs were still new to me of course, and I'd not had the time and experience Bock had.

But my timing was just fine as I sent two orbs through the support beam, down into the ground, under the home, then over to and directly under Bock's feet.

It was his turn to go airborne.

A look of shock and surprise came over his face as he flew up and backward, arms pinwheeling, legs flailing.

With his clothes now matted to his skin with rain, he impacted an old, dead pine tree. High up, where the main trunk split into two separate trunks. Even in death, it was a majestic tree. But Bock's impact shattered it, the two upper trunks pulverizing and falling to the ground, the main trunk splitting all the way to the ground. As if lightening had struck it.

He carried on through the air for a while before impacting the now muddy ground. The splash he made was a good one, though it probably wouldn't have gone over very well in an Olympic diving event.

Bock recovered quickly, pushing himself up and out of the mud, his black hair now matted to his skull and running with dirty water.

An accompanying crash of thunder to a blinding flash of lightening was immediate and severe. The ground shook with tremors as the storm, now directly overhead, was at full rage.

The wind in my face pulled my hair and beard back over my shoulders. Fat raindrops now impacted my face and dripped from eyelashes and nose.

But I paid it no mind. Instead, through the vision of the *Imminence*, I watched as Bock made his way back towards the house, all the while scanning left and right. "Rider!" he bellowed over the wind and rain, his face contorted in rage. "You think you can beat me? Me?" he roared.

But I paid no mind to his words either. Instead I studied the huge pine trunk left behind after his impact. It was massive, perhaps three feet in diameter and twenty feet high.

Bock walked passed it as he returned to the house.

I timed an orb just right. Lightening flashed and I sent a single orb to the base of the tree. The explosion was hidden perfectly in a jagged crack of thunder.

The tree trunk began to fall, but I used two more Seer orbs to control its decent. With immense concentration I lowered the massive trunk parallel with the ground, hovering about three feet above it.

Then, with every ounce of *Imminence* power I could muster, I launched it at Bock.

Through the rain and wind and darkened day, the two ton trunk closed on Bock like a giant scythe.

When it was about twenty feet away, he sensed it, sensed something sinister and powerful bearing down, and he turned.

He was fast, I had to admit that, but not fast enough. He quickly raised his own orb and sent it forward, then raised his hands across his face.

The explosion was calamitous, with two tons of tree suddenly exploding into two tons of shattered wood and splinters.

And Bock was lost in the whirlwind of it all.

The wind and rain continued its assault, helping the airborne tree fragments settle quickly to the ground.

And I waited.

A hole had been rent in the earth and had I so chosen, I could have moved closer to look down, but I dared not. I'd caught Bock off-guard twice now and I felt sure he would not let that happen again.

And I waited and watched.

I could have stood there, thinking of the loss of Lady, but I did not. History is full of dead people who let their guard down.

The rain continued to pour down unrelenting, the wind continued to slam it into my face. But I did not move.

I just watched the hole. And waited.

There was another flash of lightening, but the resulting thunder took several seconds to reach my ears. The bulk of the storm was moving away. Now it was all about the clouds bleeding out their remaining moisture. Such were summer storms in Florida, powerful and intense, but short lived.

I kept my hands firmly on the old post, the vision from the *Imminence* still locked on the crater. I could see thin rivulets of muddy water snaking over the edge of the pit, traveling how deep, I did not know.

And still I watched.

And I didn't have much longer to wait.

One hand, then two arose from the edge of the open pit and grabbed mud and flattened weeds. They were bloodied, but unbroken fingers found a hold, and I saw them strain.

First a sagging head appeared, then shoulders, then a chest. Once high enough, Bock flopped forward, his upper body slapping down on the muddy mess around the crater.

I could see his body rise and fall with breathing, then he used his hands and arms to completely extract himself. He lay there a moment, then pushed himself up on hands and knees before rocking back on his heels.

Then he lifted his head and, with a bloody smile on his face, said, "Well done, Rider." But it was more of a pained whisper than a strong, confident voice. "But we're not done yet, not yet."

The rain was slacking off a bit, but it still came down hard enough to wash the blood and dirt from his face. There were several open gashes on his cheeks and forehead, and his denim jacket was now in shreds.

And his white shirt was no longer white.

And still I watched. Stayed on the defensive. Stayed vigilant.

But I was not prepared for what he did next. I thought I'd seen the extent of his powers.

I was wrong.

But a few minutes later, when I was lying in the rubble, both of us about to die, I did not chastise myself. How could I have seen the amount of power that was about to be unleashed? The *Imminence* certainly didn't tell me.

So I was not prepared when Bock suddenly summoned not one, but two black swirling chrome orbs, leaned forward and slammed them into the ground. He did so with almost a manic laughter.

As before, the earth rose up, but not as a wave this time, but as a tsunami. The speed of its growth from the drenched soil was terrifying, like a black dragon rising from the netherworld.

But, oddly, I did not stand there and look to see how big it got. Instead, a memory recalled to the front of my mind.

Waves.

Like in water.

The top part, above the surface, folds easily around stationary objects.

But underwater, under the surface, not so much.

Meet the wave underwater, widely enough, you steal most of its power.

All of this came back from my high school science class in less than a second. Mr. Jefferson would have been proud.

So again, with no time to hesitate I sent two more orbs

with all the energy I could muster, sending them into the ground to meet the oncoming wave.

And they collided under the house.

The old home didn't stand a chance at the resulting cataclysm, and neither did I. Instead of the home exploding, it imploded as massive geysers of rock and dirt shot in all directions from under the thick, rock foundation. Remove several dozen tons of earth from under a structure, there's only one way to go.

I may have well been in the heart of a hurricane. The floor fell out from underneath me as the aged wood home imploded in upon itself as it fell through the sudden space underneath it. My eyes reflexively closed from the whirlwind of debris, but I could not shut my ears from the sound equal to ten locomotives thundering down around me. The noise was excruciating.

And then I was swallowed alive.

I do not remember coming to a landing. I do not remember the sudden stillness and quietness in the air. I do not remember the rain finally stopping. But at some point I opened my eyes to see a dark, gray sky above me, and my peripheral vision could see the rim of the giant crater I now lay in the middle of. I could also hear debris settling, finding final resting places.

I lay there in stunned silence for a while, trying to clear the fog from my head and piece together what had happened. It came eventually, if grudgingly.

Once my head was clear I focused on my body. Another damage control check. Hands and arms? Check. Move my head? Check. Move my legs?

Not so much.

I thought at first it was because my legs were trapped under rubble, but even then I should have feeling in them, and I did not.

I have never in my life experienced true panic. Trepidation and fear, sure, like the first time I parachuted out of an airplane in Ranger school, but never hysteria or panic. But now, as I lay there, not being able to move or feel my legs, panic did indeed raise its ugly head as I raised mine slightly to look towards my lower extremities; and realized that not feeling my legs was the least of my worries.

Protruding up through my abdomen was a spear of wood, perhaps a piece of wall lattice. It only stuck up a couple inches, but was covered with gore, and I knew there had to be an entry point, namely somewhere through my lower back.

Oddly, there was no pain.

I looked at it sternly, as if my blue-eyed stare would make it go away, make it feel guilty and sorry for hurting me in this way, make it rife with shame.

But of course this didn't work, and I never considered it would. So I laid my head back down and stared at the sky. There were white and gray clouds up there, roiling against one another, fighting between themselves to see who would become cumulus clouds, or stratus, or nimbus, or whatever kind of clouds follow storms. I don't really know, I'm not a weather guy. Perhaps I could have been, had it not been for the *Imminence*.

So I stared at the sky and, as my Ranger training demanded, began flipping through solutions to my current situation. There was always an answer, we were taught, always a way to survive if you tried. And though Rangers are always thought of as brawn, it really was more about brains. Brawn's without brains, you were dead. Brains without brawn's – well – you stood a better chance, but nothing was better than both combined, in good proportions.

But the fact was, things didn't look good. I was probably bleeding internally, and I for sure couldn't walk, much less drag myself out of this crater with just arms and hands. And I was quite sure Bock, if he was still around, wasn't going to call 911 for me. And even if he did the nearest hospital was what, twenty miles away? More? And how long would it take them to extract me from this pit? They'd need at least a medivac chopper.

No, things did not look good at all.

So I laid there and looked at the sky, and wondered. I thought of my parents and all they did for me. I thought of Lady T and the endless highways and byways we'd traveled together. I thought of Bopper and Cora and the many other friends I'd made in the travels of my life.

And I thought of Dara, a young girl who, in just a few short hours, had become something of a kid sister to me. I even went shopping with her after all. In a pink frou-frou store laden with perfume to boot.

Yes, I would indeed miss Dara.

But I didn't dwell on these things overly. I lived my life the best I could, as honestly as I could. I had no regrets and the Clearing comes for everyone soon enough.

It seemed it was my turn.

When a lightheaded fuzziness began to overtake me, I heard a noise, far to my left. It pulled me out of the fog for a moment and I turned my head towards the sound.

Bock. Standing at the edge of the crater. Looking down at me. "Wow," he hollered, but it sounded weak and labored. "You're tough, Rider. Made it through all that, huh?"

I said nothing and Bock began a long, laborious journey down the crater wall. I watched him all the way, picking and stumbling through boards and overturned trees, around sheets of steel roofing and piles of cracked stone masonry that had once been the foundation of the home.

Eventually he arrived at my side, bloodied and exhausted; clothing shredded and filthy; hair still muddy and caked to his

239

skull. He looked at me and smiled, then dropped to his knees about ten feet away and just sat there awhile, breathing hard. "You don't look so good, Rider," he said in between deep breaths. His eyes flicked to the shaft of wood sticking out of my gut. "But that was kind of fun, yes?"

I didn't reply, just looked at him. I wanted to cough, but I knew if I did I would probably cough up blood. Perhaps the stake had punctured my lower right lung. Plus, I didn't want to give him the satisfaction.

Bock sat back on his heels and just smiled. Then he raised a hand and, with some effort in his face, summoned an orb. Smaller this time, and only one, but it was of swirling black chrome.

There was only one thing left to do, I thought, and summoned my own two small orbs. At least my hands were free of rubble.

Bock cackled. "What? Not done yet?" he asked and laughed for a moment. Then he said, "I've got to hand it to you, Rider, you're one tough bastard." Then the smile went away and he stated, "But it's over now."

I looked at him for a long moment and summoned the strength to talk without coughing. "I don't think so," I said, then did the one thing your not supposed to do with the Seer Orbs. I imagined Dayton was cringing in his seat as I brought my hands together.

A look of horror flashed across Bock's face. "No!" he screamed, trying to jump and stop me, but it was too late.

I turned my eyes back skyward and looked at the clouds as I brought my hands, and the orbs, together in a thundering clap.

Tampa Bay Picayune

Wednesday, August 12th, 2014

Kess Powers - Reporting

From Tampa Bay – Police and the EPA are investigating an inland explosion that occurred north of I-4 and about twenty miles east of Tampa Bay. The explosion happened at the Lower Green Swamp Preserve, a currently shut down historical site due to the sluggish economy. No one is allowed in the vicinity for safety reasons, according to an inside source, but it looks initially like an underground natural gas explosion caused by an intense lightening storm that passed through the area yesterday morning. It is reported that the resulting crater is almost a quarter mile wide, though that can't be confirmed at this time. There are no reported injuries, though a demolished motorcycle was found nearby. Visit TampaBayPicayune.Com for more information and further details as they are released.

Tampa Bay Picayune

Wednesday, August 12th, 2014

Kurt Gains - Reporting

From Tampa Bay – There was quite a commotion in the sleepy neighborhood of Suncoast Marina yesterday morning. Retirees and their loved ones were awakened by numerous police cars and SWAT team trucks as they swarmed their neighborhood, eventually converging on the marina itself. Offshore, numerous police interceptor boats converged on a single boat that had just docked.

Police are not currently releasing information, but the boat and crew were taken into custody, then the entire marina neighborhood was forcibly evacuated.

One inside source reports that canisters of ricin were discovered on board the vessel, but that cannot be confirmed at this time. The Chief of Police will give a statement today at noon from City Hall.

Afterward

Les Carraway sat behind the reception desk at Sarasota Triumph Motorcycles. It was a Monday morning, and on Monday mornings people were not thinking about buying motorcycles, Triumph or otherwise. Instead they were grumbling through traffic and slurping their Starbucks coffees and counting the hours till Friday.

So Les picked through the few sales that came through over the weekend. A Speedmaster, two Thunderbirds and one Daytona. Not bad for off-season in Florida. He'd seen worse.

But Monday's were typically a slow day, so slow in fact that Les ran his business without service technicians or extra salespeople. He'd be lucky to even have a looky-loo on a Monday. He'd read somewhere that male testosterone levels build as the week progressed, so usually by Friday guys started to come in, investigating what Triumph could offer that Harley Davidson could not.

In truth, both motorcycles were excellent, it just depended on what felt right on the road. Both companies had been around for a long, long time. Both companies built bikes with pride.

Les knew Harley had the upper hand, no doubt, but Triumph was slowly taking its fair share with quality, reliability and service after the sale. Les was a salesman at heart and always saw the silver lining.

After reviewing the weekend's sales, he dropped his pen on the desk. The thunk sound echoed throughout the sales floor.

And then he saw him, a man walk into the parking lot.

He wore black denim jeans and a blue denim shirt and a black leather jacket. Pretty warm clothing for August in Florida, but Les didn't think on it too much. He watched with a salesman's eye as the man looked over a few used bikes in the lot and, one at a time, reject them.

Then the man came inside. He was a huge man, pushing six foot five and probably tipping the scales at two forty or two fifty. His hair was short and sun bleached. His beard looked about five days old. The size of his chest looked like a Sherman tank.

"Morning," Les said casually. The man looked up and nodded in return.

He looked over some bikes at the front of the store, and Les didn't interrupt him. He was seasoned enough to know that an immediate in-your-face greeting and pushy salesmanship was the best way to lose a sale. So he let the man wander for a few minutes.

And the man did. He looked over a Speedmaster, then a Daytona, then moved off. He wandered up and down the small isles of bikes with thumbs hooked through belt loops, and then he stopped and reached out.

He put his hand on the gas tank of a Triumph Rocket 3, the Touring Edition. It was all screaming chrome and flame red, with hardwall saddlebags, the Triumph logo on their sides. And it had fat, black tires. And a radiator at the front of the engine. And it had a two thousand, two hundred, ninety four cubic centimeter liquid-cooled engine with five speeds. It had one hundred forty six horses with which to pull asphalt.

It had a double-overhead-cam in-line three cylinder engine. Not a little boy's bike.

Then the man looked up at Les, and his storm blue eyes caught him off guard for a moment. "Nice ride," Les said, remaining seated. "Most powerful production motorcycle in the world."

"What's the fuel economy?"

"City or highway?"

"Highway, always highway."

"Average, forty five."

The man nodded. "How much?" he asked.

"For you? Twenty grand even. And I'll throw in a helmet

of your choosing for free."

The man nodded and looked back down at the gleaming monstrosity. "Cash discount?" the man asked.

"What percentage?"

"All of it. And I mean the green stuff, not plastic."

Les's ears perked up and he leaned forward. "Seventeen five and you can ride off in less than an hour."

The man looked up, his eyes piercing. "Sixteen five and you still throw in the helmet."

Les thought for a moment, but just for show. "Deal," he said.

Then the man walked up to his desk, pulled a massive roll of bills out of his jacket pocket and slowly counted off one hundred sixty hundred dollar bills. Les piled them up as the man flicked them onto the table, one at a time.

"I want a full tank of gas too," the man said when he was done. "And take the windshield off, I like the wind in my face." Then they did the paperwork.

*   *   *

Somewhere, out there, on a lone, darkened Florida highway, the newly christened Lady R purred like an iron jaguar as she pulled blackish-gray asphalt from the future, into the present, and out to the past.

The rider kept the throttle steady for a long time, just cruising along, feeling the engine, watching dashed yellow lines flash by, enjoying the cool night air rushing through his helmet.

But eventually the rider reached a road that he knew to be long, and open, and straight, and free of any hiding places for police cars. "Let's see what the Lady's got," he mumbled into his helmet. So he gave the throttle a little twist, and the jaguar snarled in response, lashed out at the naked road, dug for purchase, parted the wind.

The rider ticked into fifth and the bike vanished into the dark, and a thundering echo faded into the night air.

Author's Note

What you hold in your hands is a complete rewrite of the original book, finished in 2011. I wrote the original edition in third person and, while editing, decided first person would have been much better. And the original version was just terribly written anyway.

So I shelved Rider for over two years and worked on other books, namely "A Geeks Life," "Meg Hunter" and the trilogy, "Pilgrimage of the Phoenix." The latter book consumed almost a year, but when I was done, I decided to undertake Rider again. He's a good man and I felt terrible having left him on a dusty shelf for so long. His story needed to be told to the world.

My father was the main motivator for this book. When my wife and I first moved to Florida I had a very difficult time finding employment so, as an encouragement, my father offered me a job: Write a book and I'll pay you per chapter. I think he wound up dishing out about a grand in the end, an amount I'll pay him back one day, just because that first edition was so bad.

Anyway, when he made the offer I did a lot of thinking. I've always liked the 'lone wolf' type of character, such as John MacDonalds' character Travis McGee, Lee Childs' Jack Reacher and Michael Connellys' Harry Bosch.

(In fact, Rider's real name, Bix, is a tip of the hat to MacDonald. A character in one of his books was named Bix, though it was a woman, and I thought it was a really nifty name.)

But at the same time, I also like science fiction and fantasy so, in the end, I kind of created an amalgam.

I hope this is the beginning of a long line of Rider books. I enjoyed writing it tremendously and feel there are a lot more adventures for Rider in the future.

Thanks for reading, I hoped you enjoyed.

MDS – January 21, 2014

Please contact the author at:
MegToothMan@Yahoo.Com

Or, join on Facebook at:
Michael Smith - Author

A Note About Self Publishing

With the recent advent of Websites such as Smashwords, Wordclay and CreateSpace, the door has swung wide open to anyone who wants to publish a book. No red tape, no publishing house hurdles to clear, no rejection letters, no fat-cat publisher who looks at you and your work and only sees dollar signs (or lack of). Though I do have to pay a fee for every book that I sell through CreateSpace, I can _sell_ _my_ _book_, not fight with hurdles and red tape and selfish, money-greedy publishers who only consider their wallets and yachts and not the writer.

There is one common drawback to self-published books though, the editing is not always so great. As doctors make the worst patients, authors make the worst editors. Me included.

It's not that budding, self-publishing authors don't _want_ to have their books professionally edited (or ghost-written), it's that most of us can't _afford_ to have it done. The average charge to have a book professionally edited hovers around five cents a word. That means I would have had to shuck out almost twenty three hundred dollars to have _Rider, The Imminence_ edited, and guess what I don't have?

You guessed it.

So I have to edit myself, or implore family and friends to help; family and friends who have busy lives of their own; work, kids, mortgage payments, school, a car that needs a new tire, a lawn to mow, a weekend Honey-Do list; you get the picture.

So while I encourage you to buy books from budding, self-publishing authors, I ask that you forgive them their minor editing issues. They're only human and, most of them, really just write for the sheer joy of writing, not to have the Editor Police chase them down every step of the way.

I and my fellow self-publishers would appreciate it.

8333379R00137

Made in the USA
San Bernardino, CA
05 February 2014